HIGH WIRE

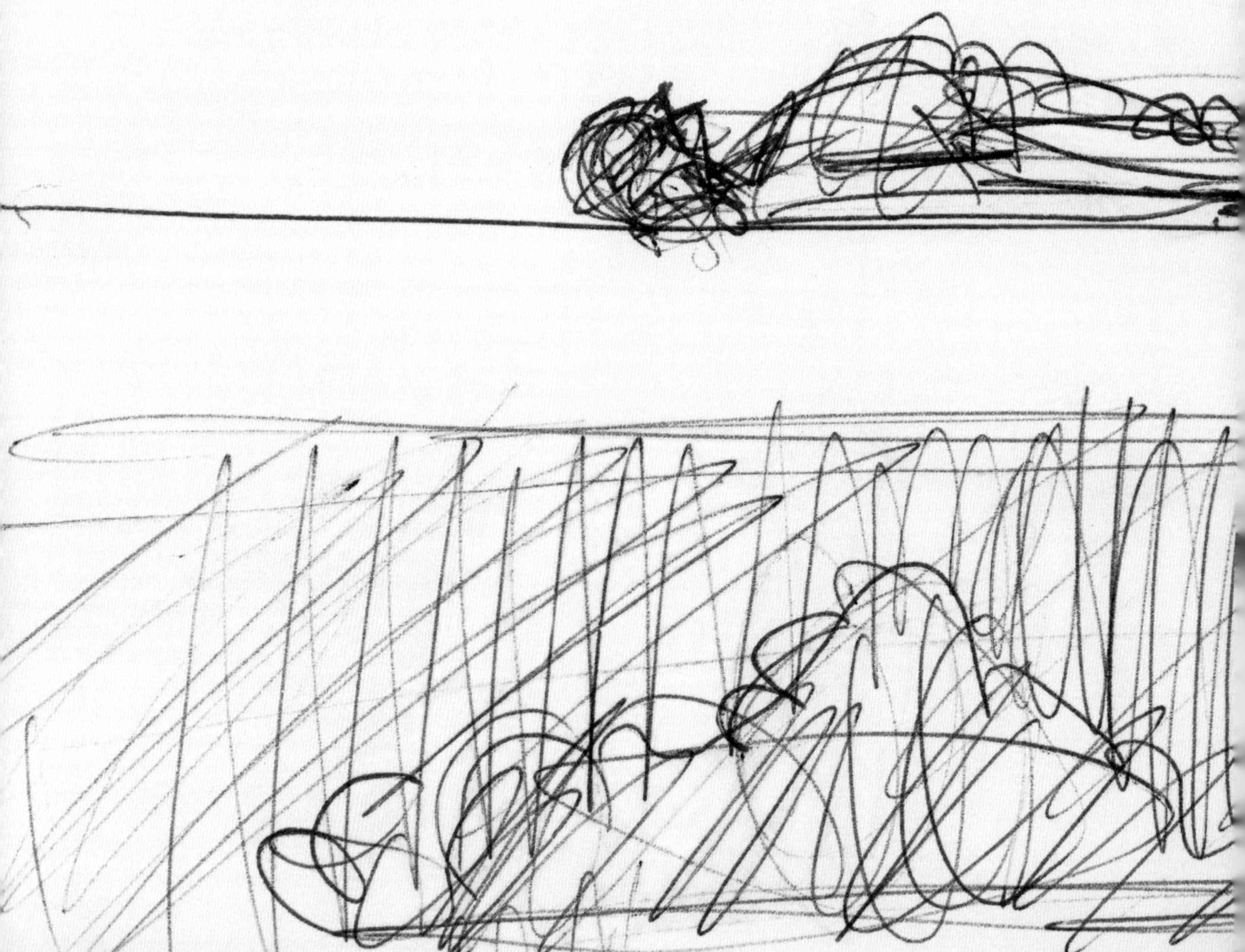

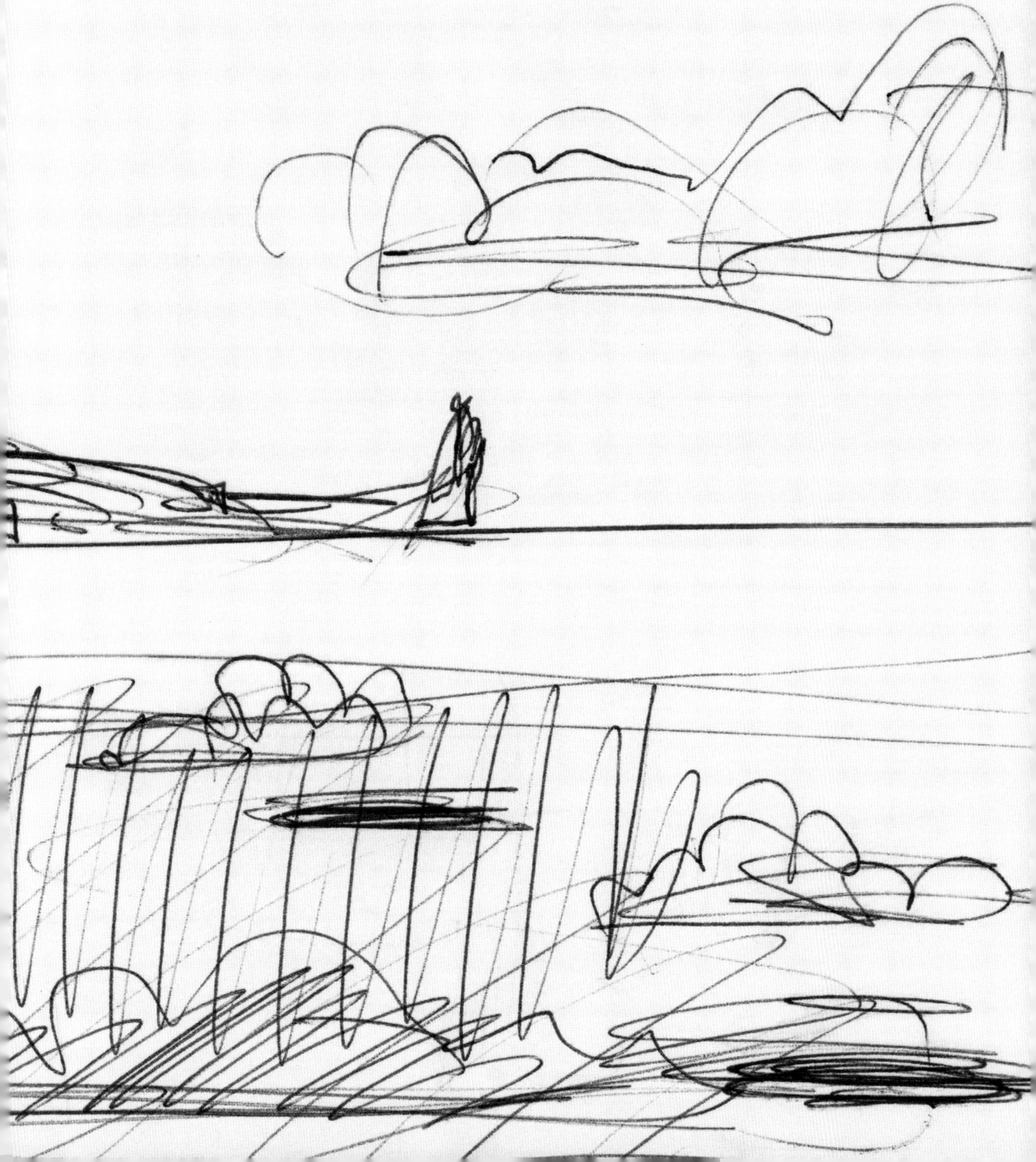

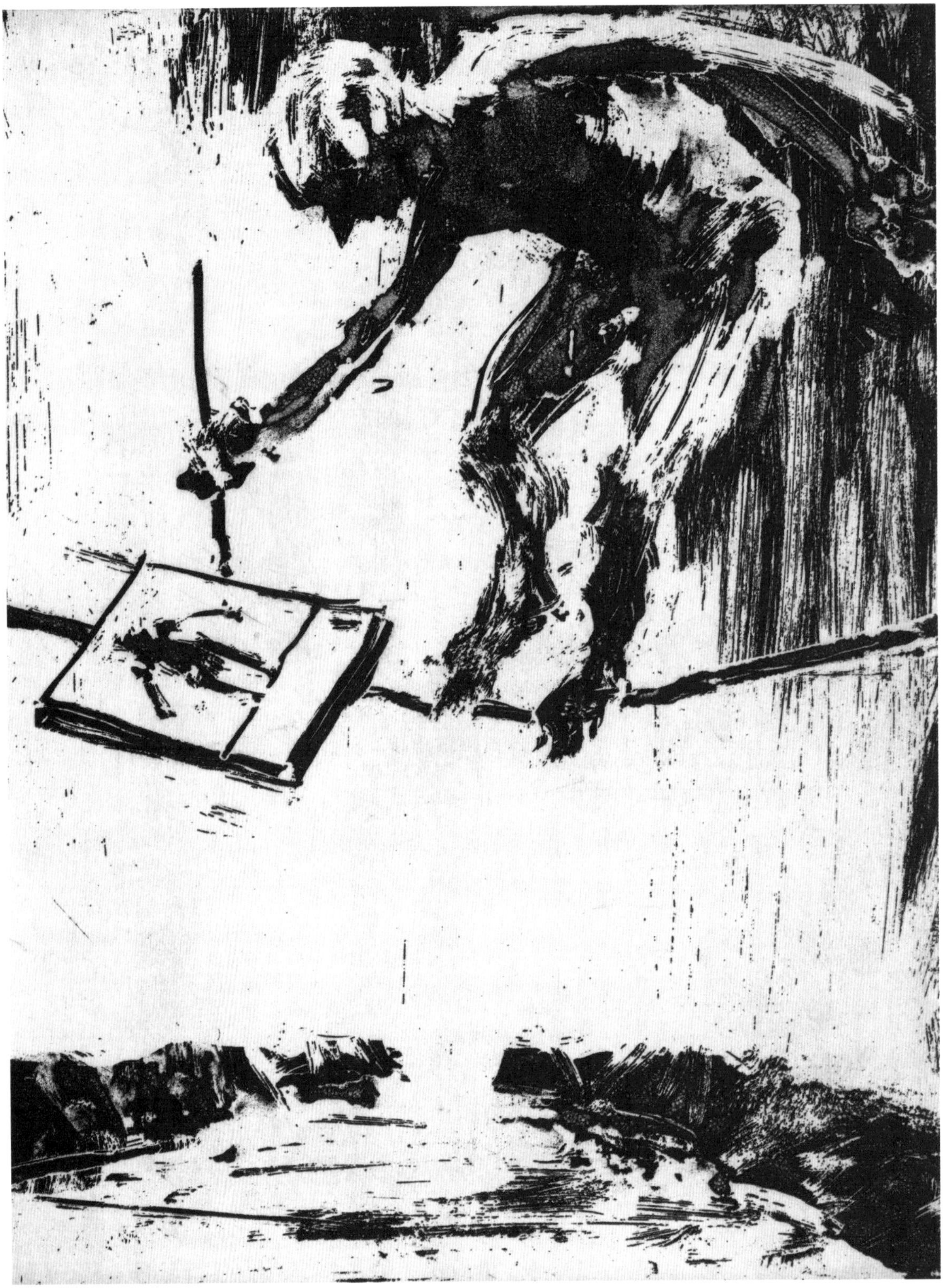

HIGH WIRE

LLOYD JONES

and

EUAN MACLEOD

MASSEY UNIVERSITY PRESS

I'd written to Euan Macleod proposing a project about bridges. He replied enthusiastically — and, over the coming months, sketches and drawings of bridges tumbled freely out of him. I began to think of a single life consisting of many bridges crossed, then re-crossed, one after another — of departures and arrivals, ascents and as many descents until at last we're alone hoisted high above the ordinary and mundane, and we've left behind all that which anchors us in time and place.

But soon the heady ideas I had about bridges began to collapse. Where I had been, others had. The commonality of experience breathed its deflating air. As exhilarating as it had been to walk across Golden Gate Bridge or to soar above Sydney Harbour or to flit across the modest rainbow from childhood, my footsteps fitted neatly into others'; my beating heart fell in with theirs.

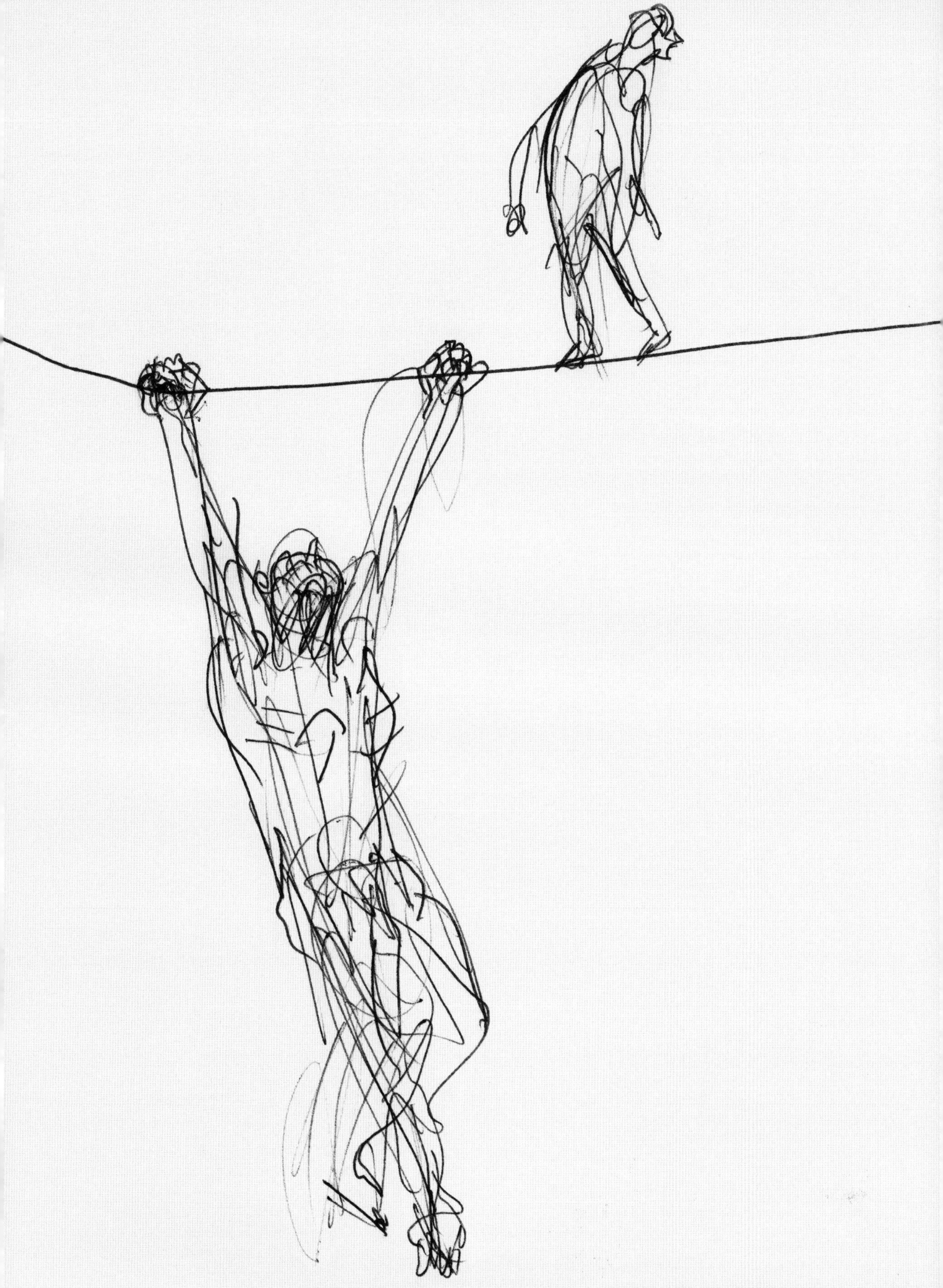

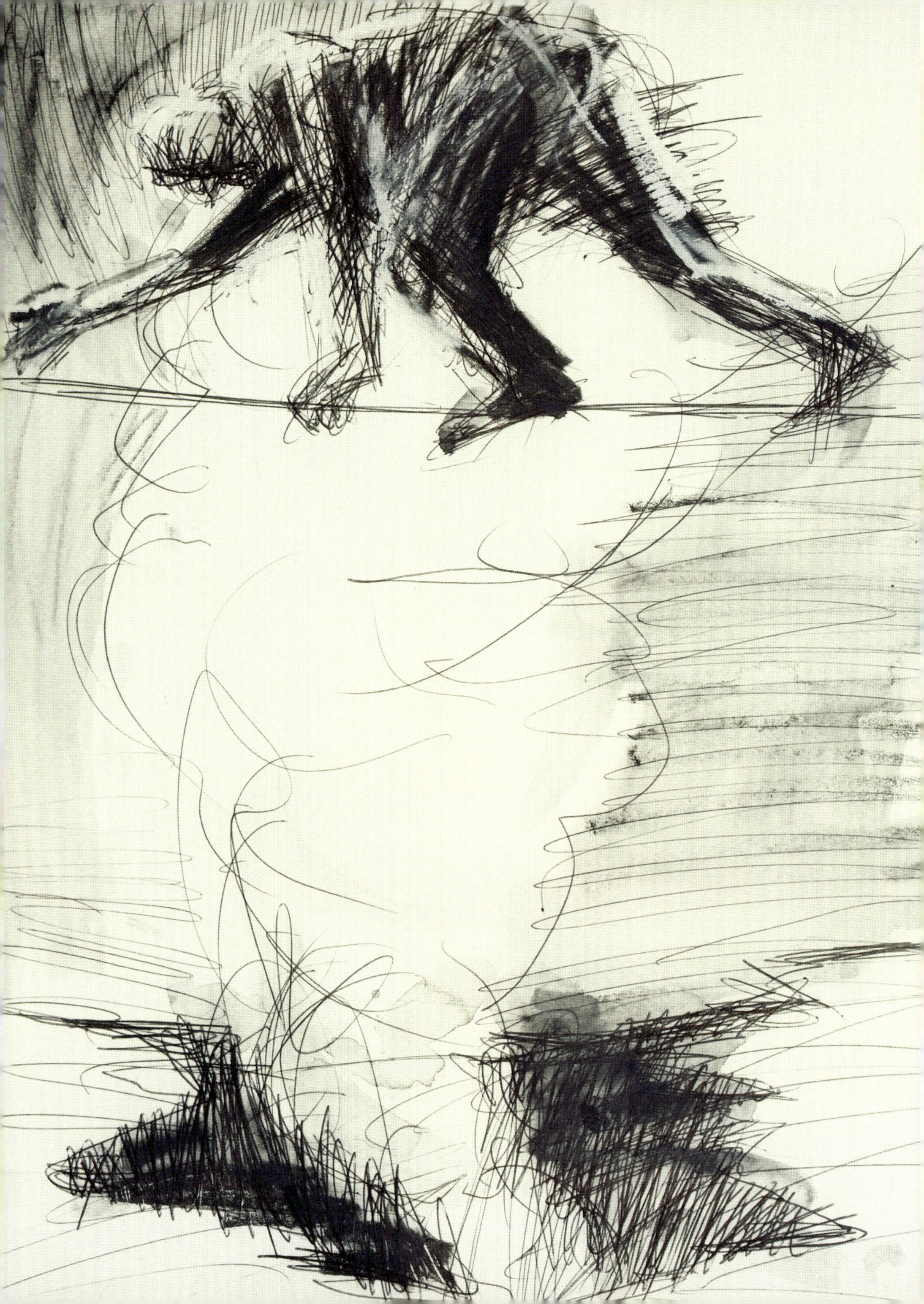

I was not where I thought I was. I was not alone. The art I looked for was not there.

Then I discovered Philippe Petit — the most daring tightroper the world has ever known. A real artist able to place his feet in a space where no one else had. Seeing a path where no one else had. And then dismantling, and tidying up after, to ensure the endeavour would not grow old inside a frame but live on through the re-telling of those who were there and saw it happen. He is an elfin twenty-four-year-old dressed in black samurai pants and a tight black v-neck vest that morning, in 1974, when he steps onto a wire linking the twin towers of the World Trade Center.

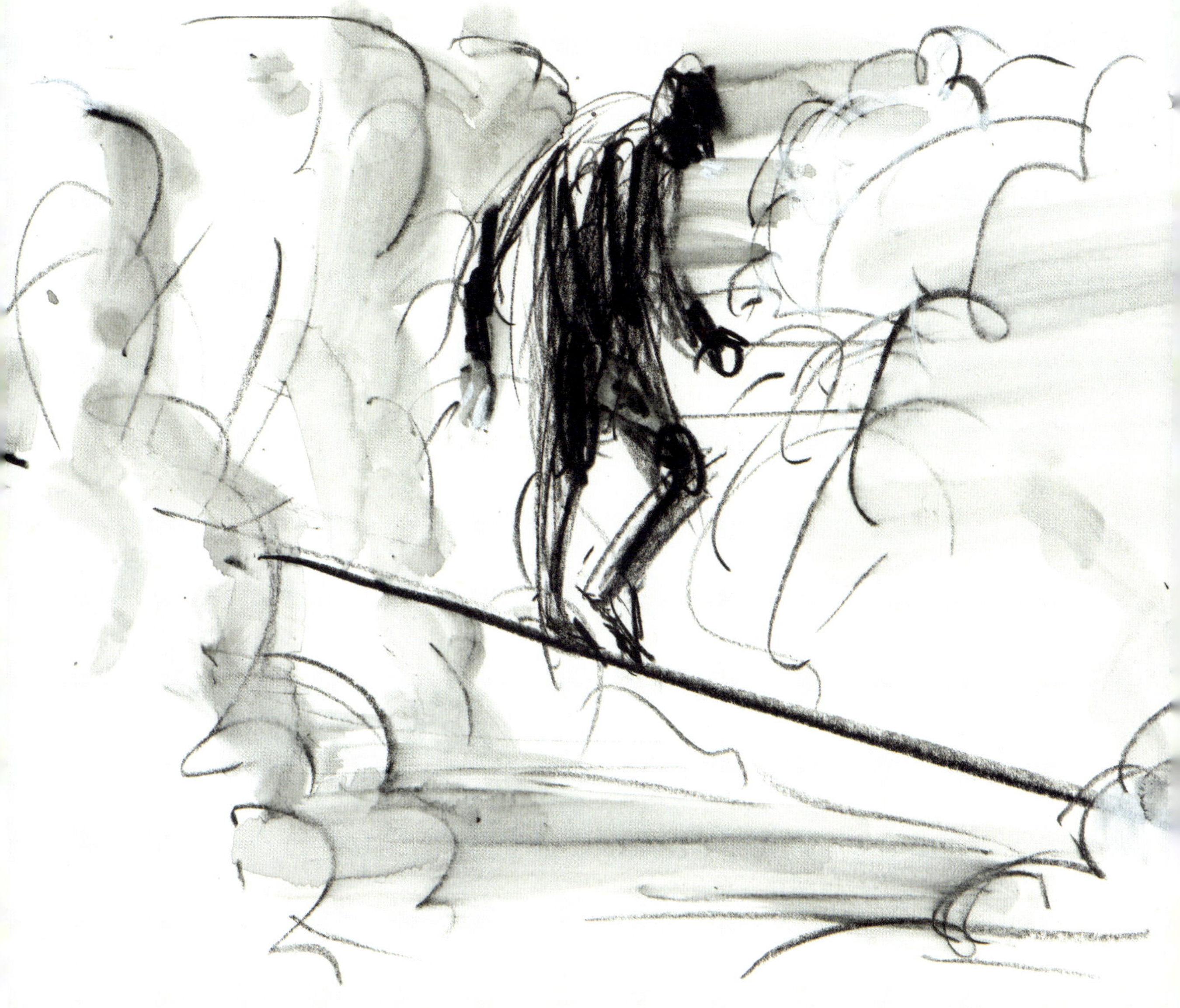

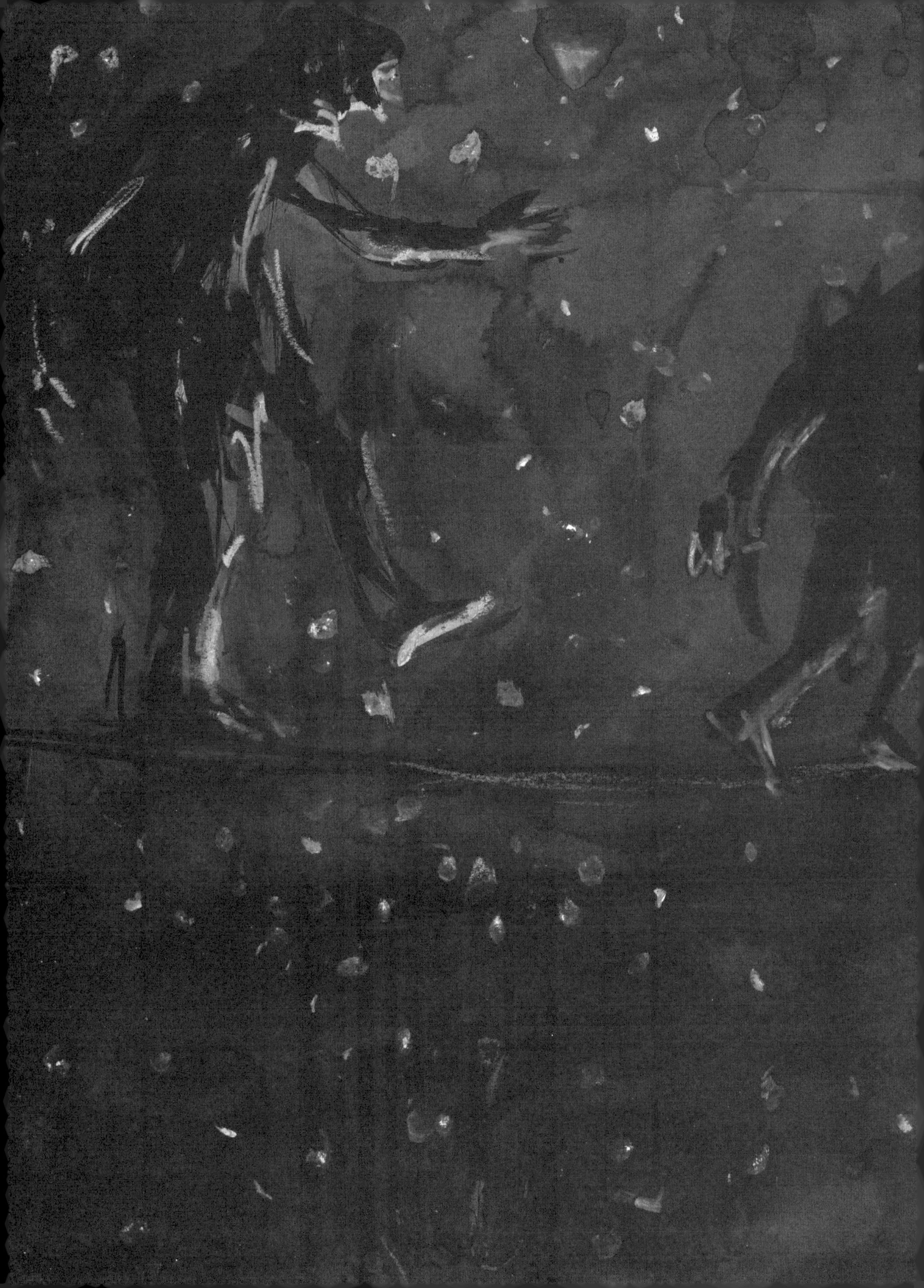

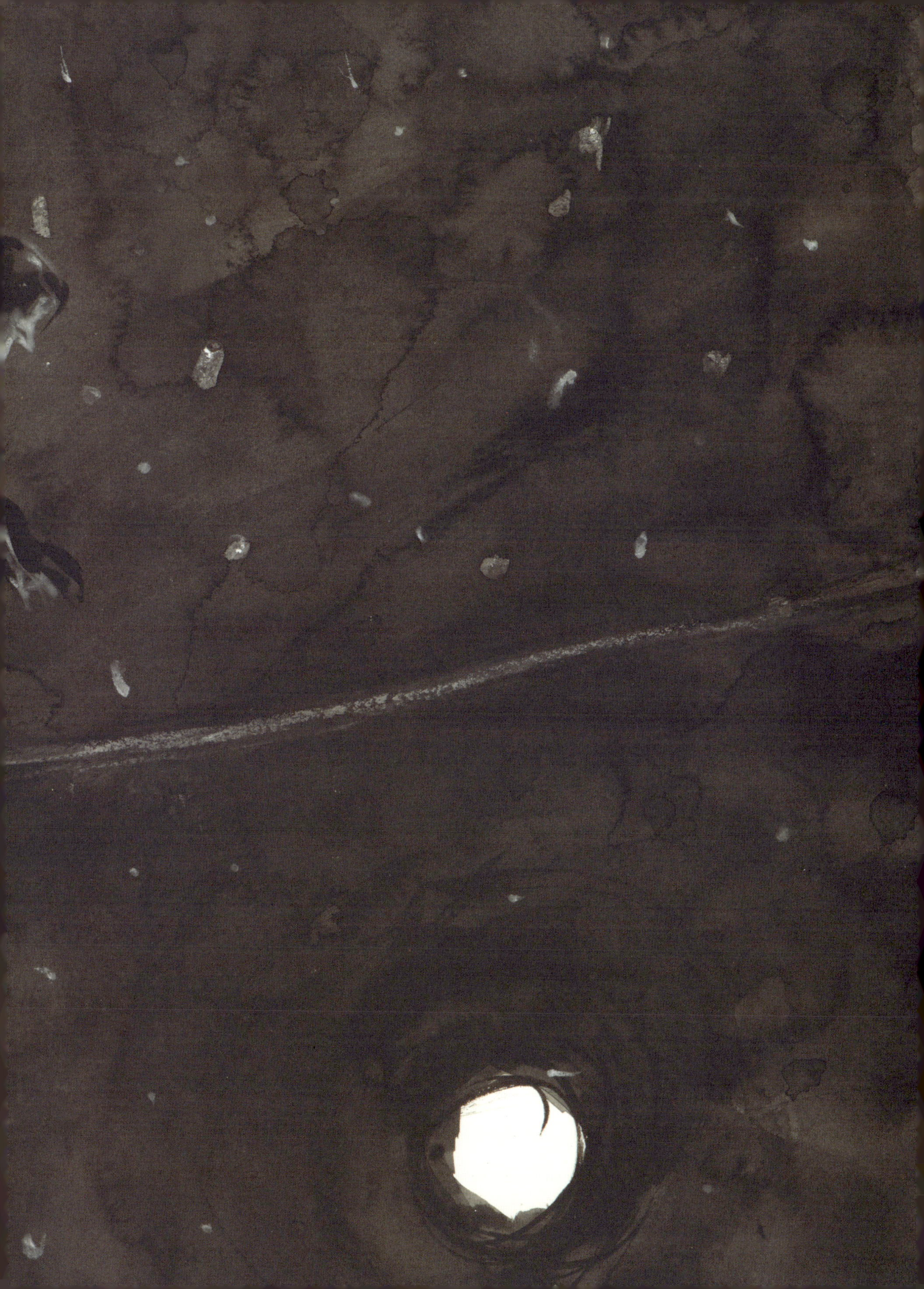

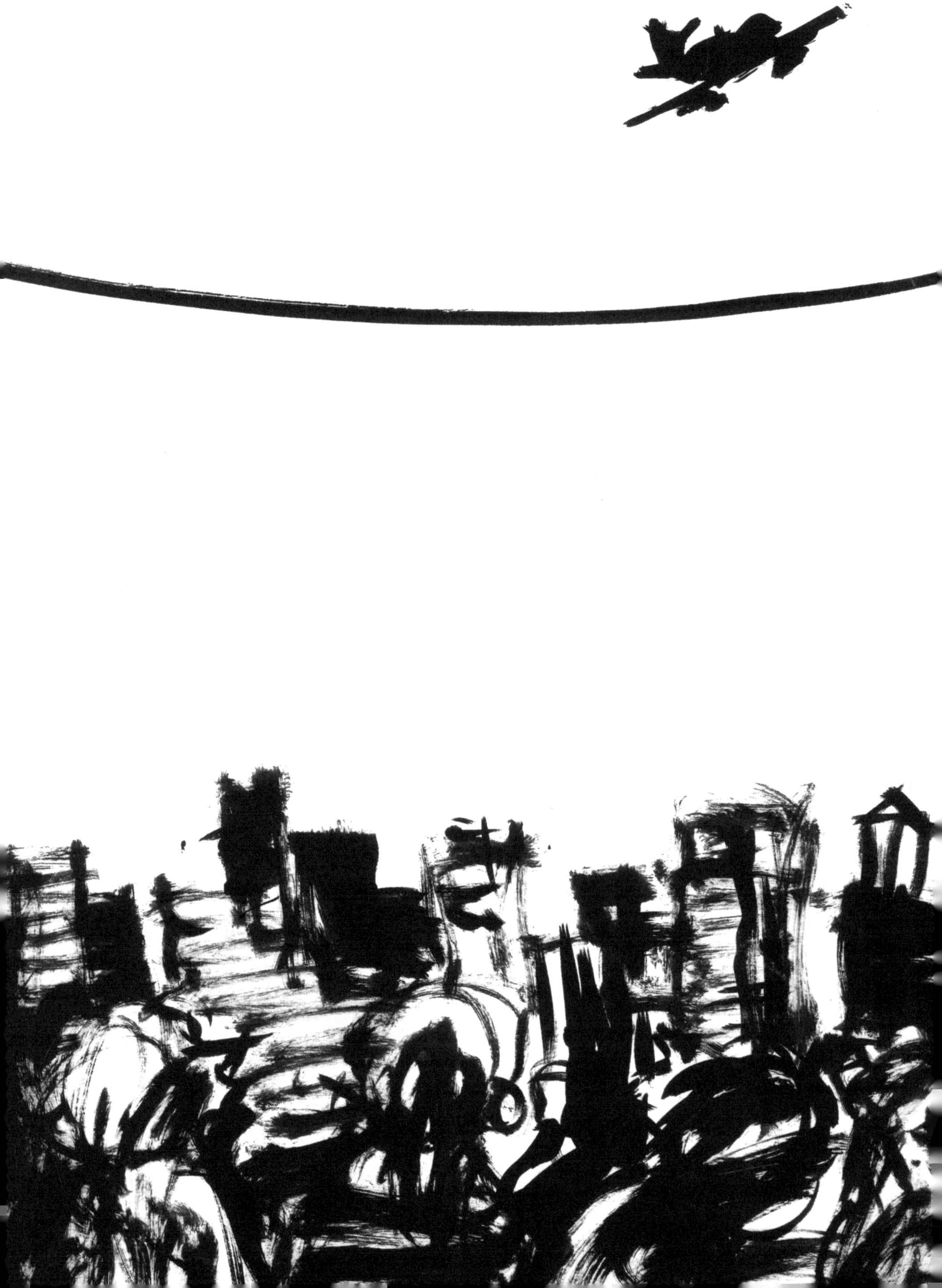

For the next forty-five minutes he walks up and down the wire; he bounces on it, he lies down on it, places his balancing pole across his chest to turn himself into a human crucifix. He dances with death. He taunts it. He flaunts our gravest fears. He perches where we would never place ourselves. And like all great artists he is totally detached from what his audience feels.

There is a photo of him lying on the wire as a Boeing flies across the slot of sky above. Decades later, that same slot of clear sky will be muddied by the two hijacked planes. The same hard glinting towers before the fire-lit apparition of a plane bursts through one, then the other.

Ten years after Petit's daring feat, I visited one of the towers. I'm not great with heights — and I was reminded of this as I nervously approached a window on the top floor, or perhaps I should say the summit, and looked down on a small plane that promptly disappeared into low cloud.

Suddenly I knew to a spine-chilling degree how high up he'd been. What courage. To trust himself, to trust the wire. To take that first step. To see a bridge where no one else had.

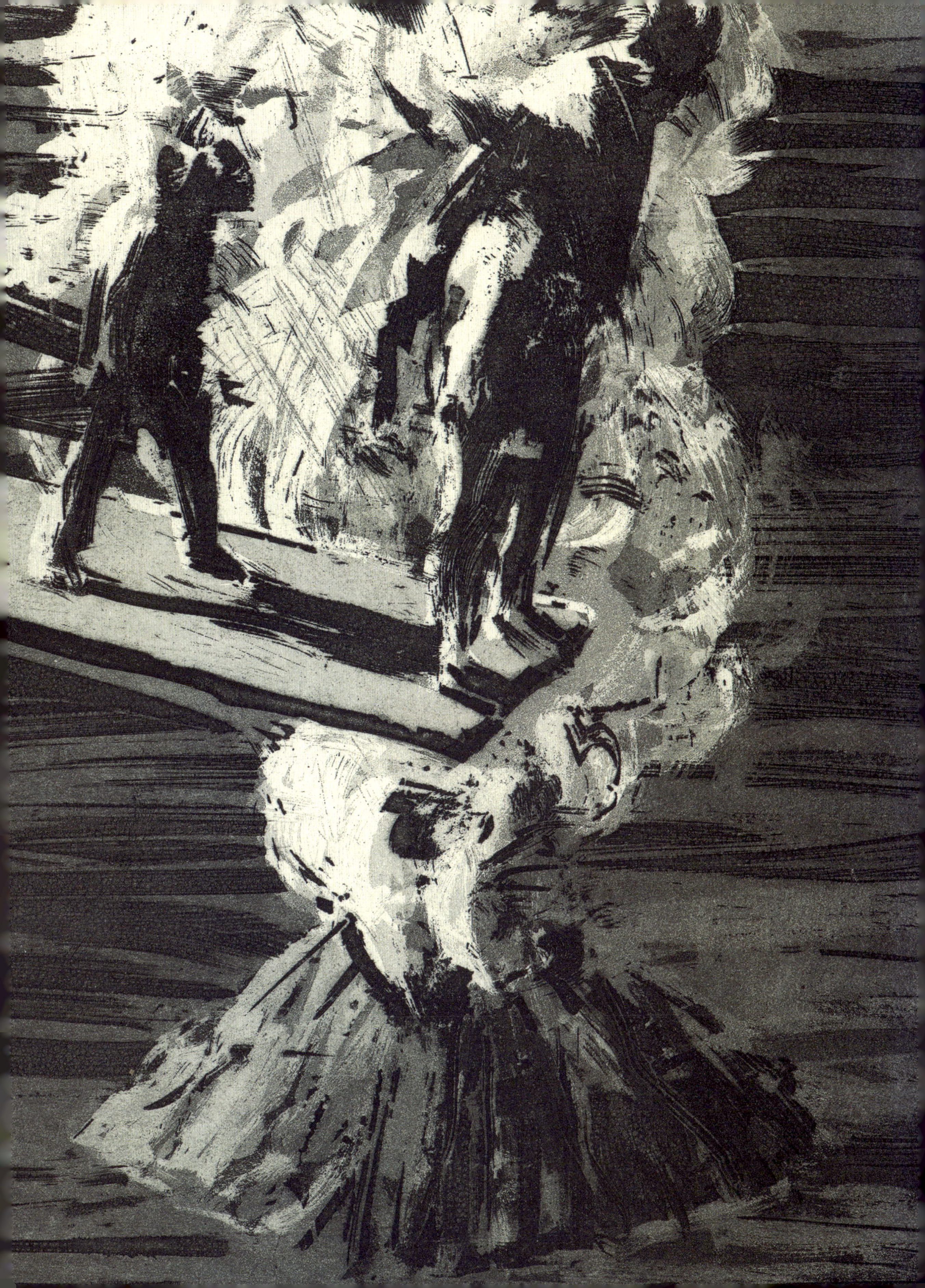

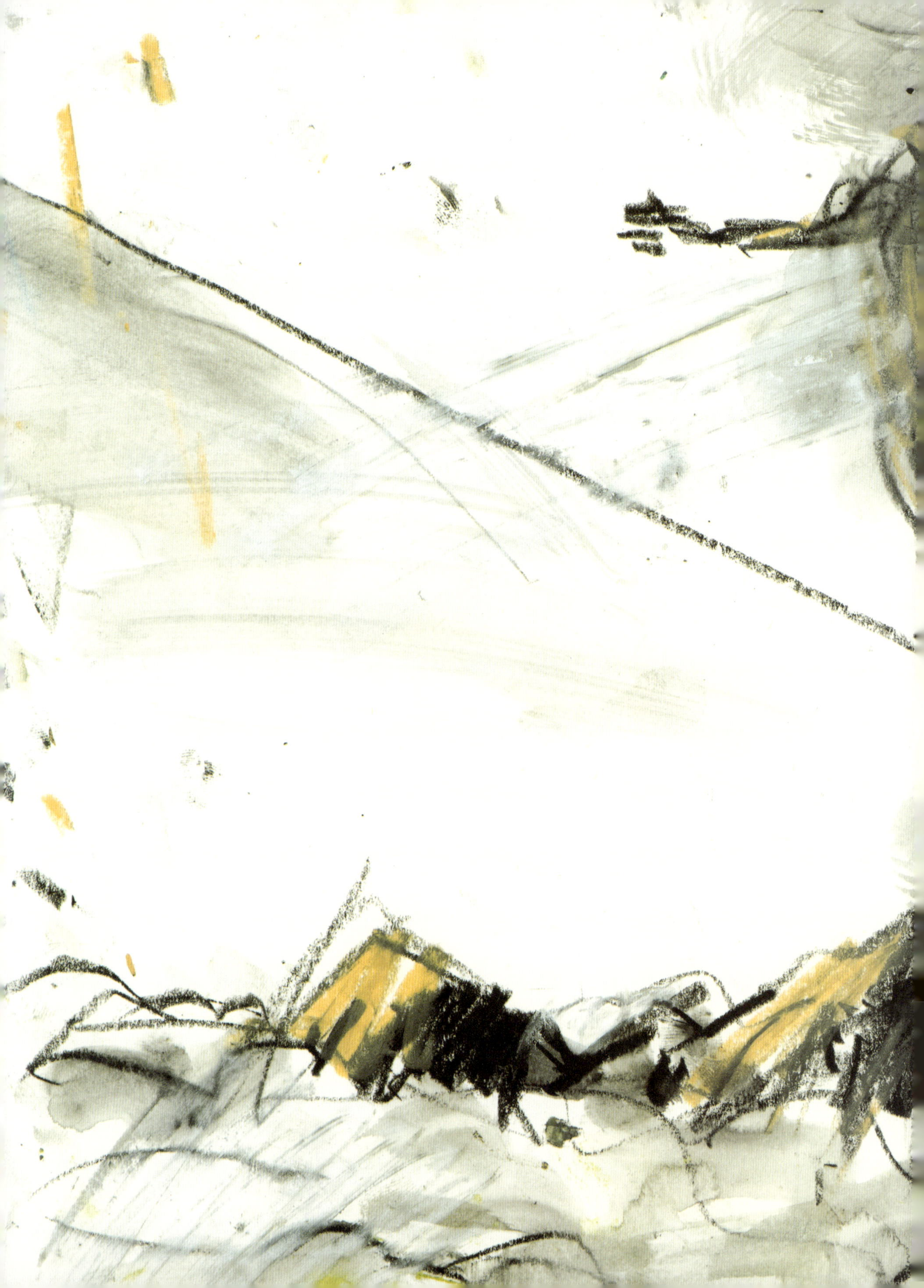

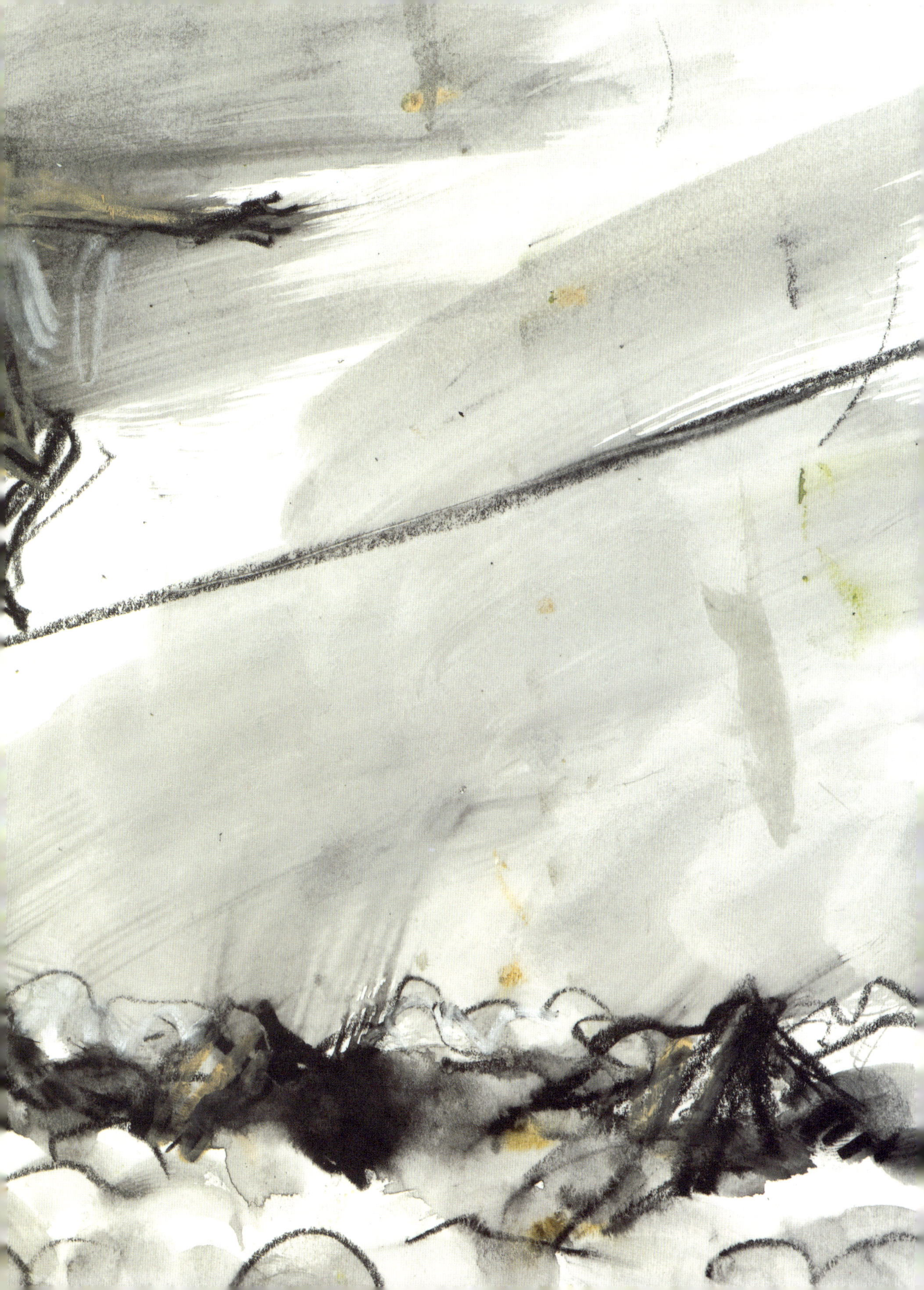

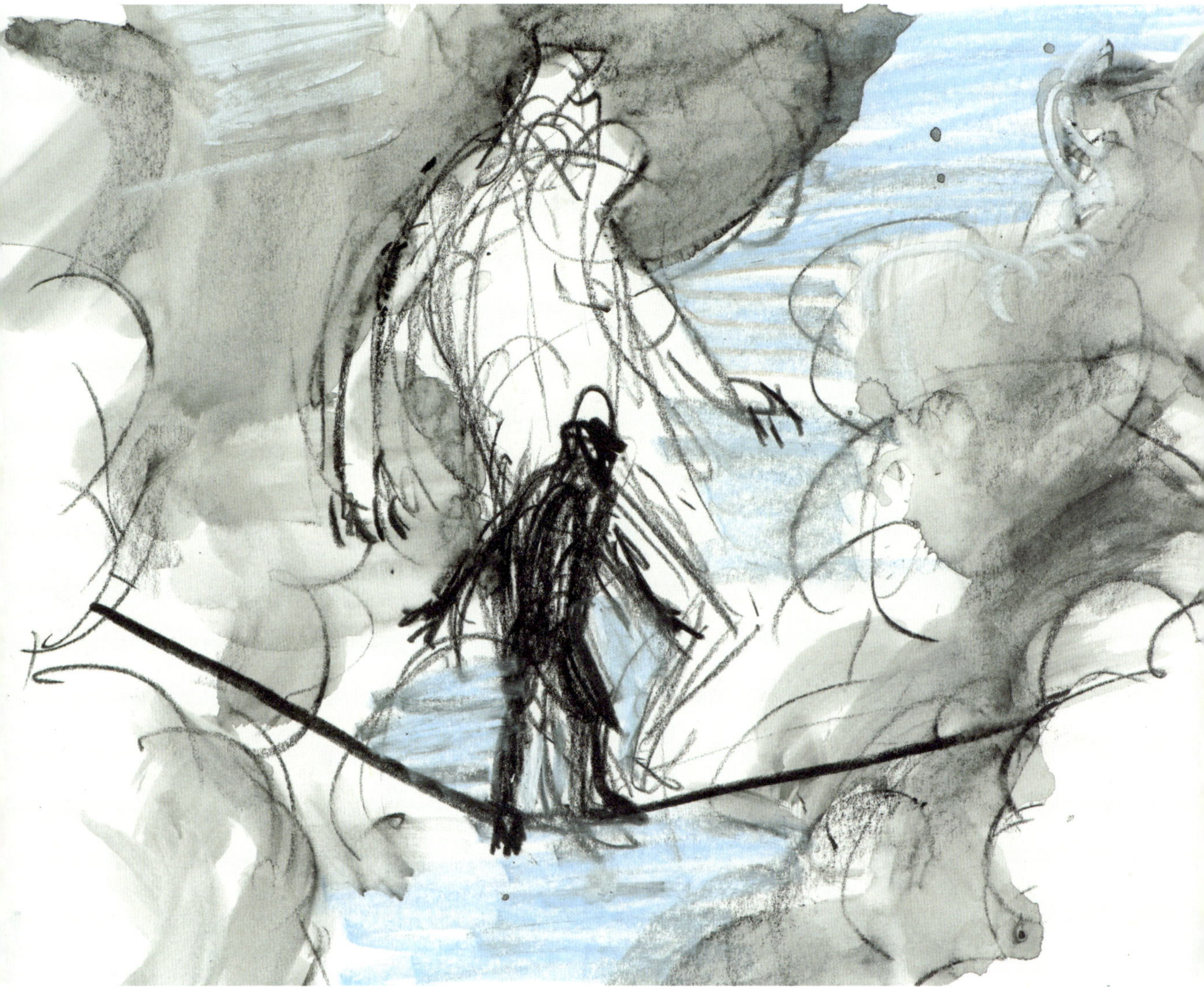

As a child, to get to the swimming pool I had to cross the railway tracks. A bridge conveyed me to that chlorinated heaven. First, the gentle ascent to where, briefly, I hovered high above the train tracks and the suburban rooftops. A bridge is an adult form, and so I felt part of an adult endeavour and, however briefly, enjoyed a confidence inspired by the genius who found a way for the road and footpath to throw me up in the air before gathering me safely on the other side.

And when I looked back where I had come from, I saw the shape of my desire rising and falling after me.

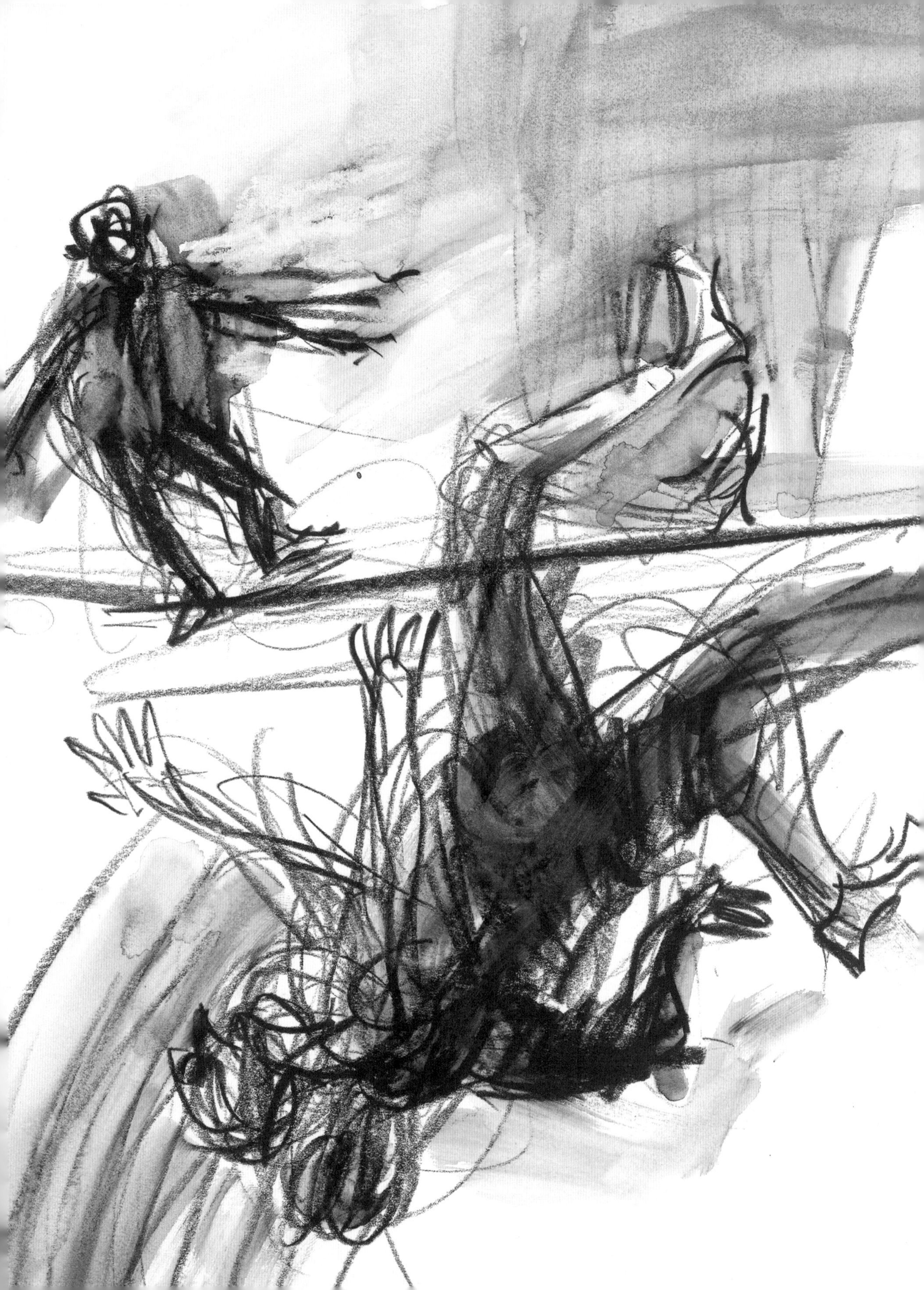

At first it is easy. There is no other way — the way is up — and all you do is place one foot after the other. The leading toe presses down for purchase, followed by a slight bodily drag which, in later years, has increased as the leading toe has started to founder with uncertainty.

The height terrifies, yet I am drawn to the edge — what to make of this curious temptation to throw myself off?

It is inexplicable. But there it is — a temptation with gravitational pull. The people I saw fall from the twin towers were those without choice. Flames licked at their backs as they chose their moment to leap.

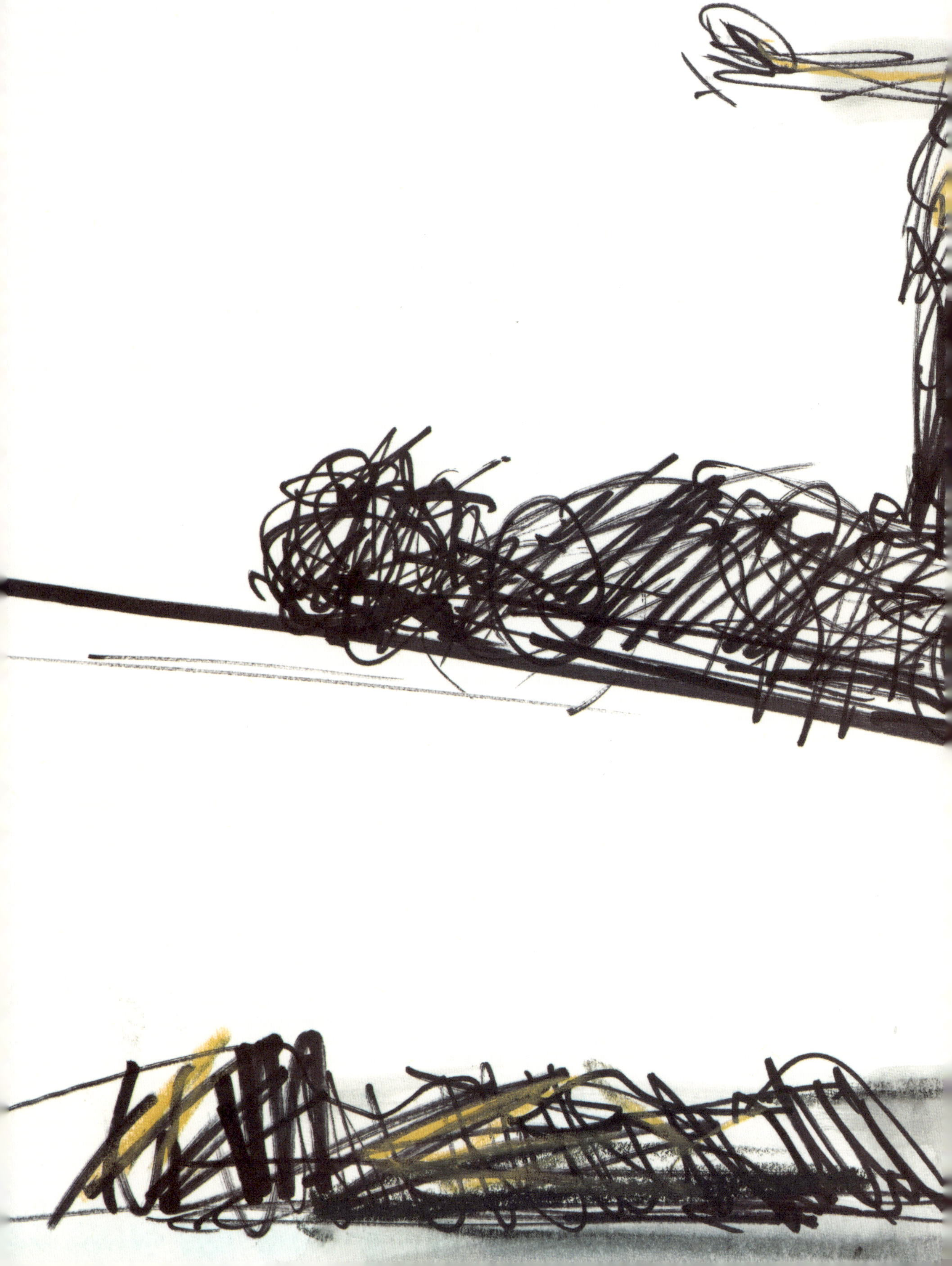

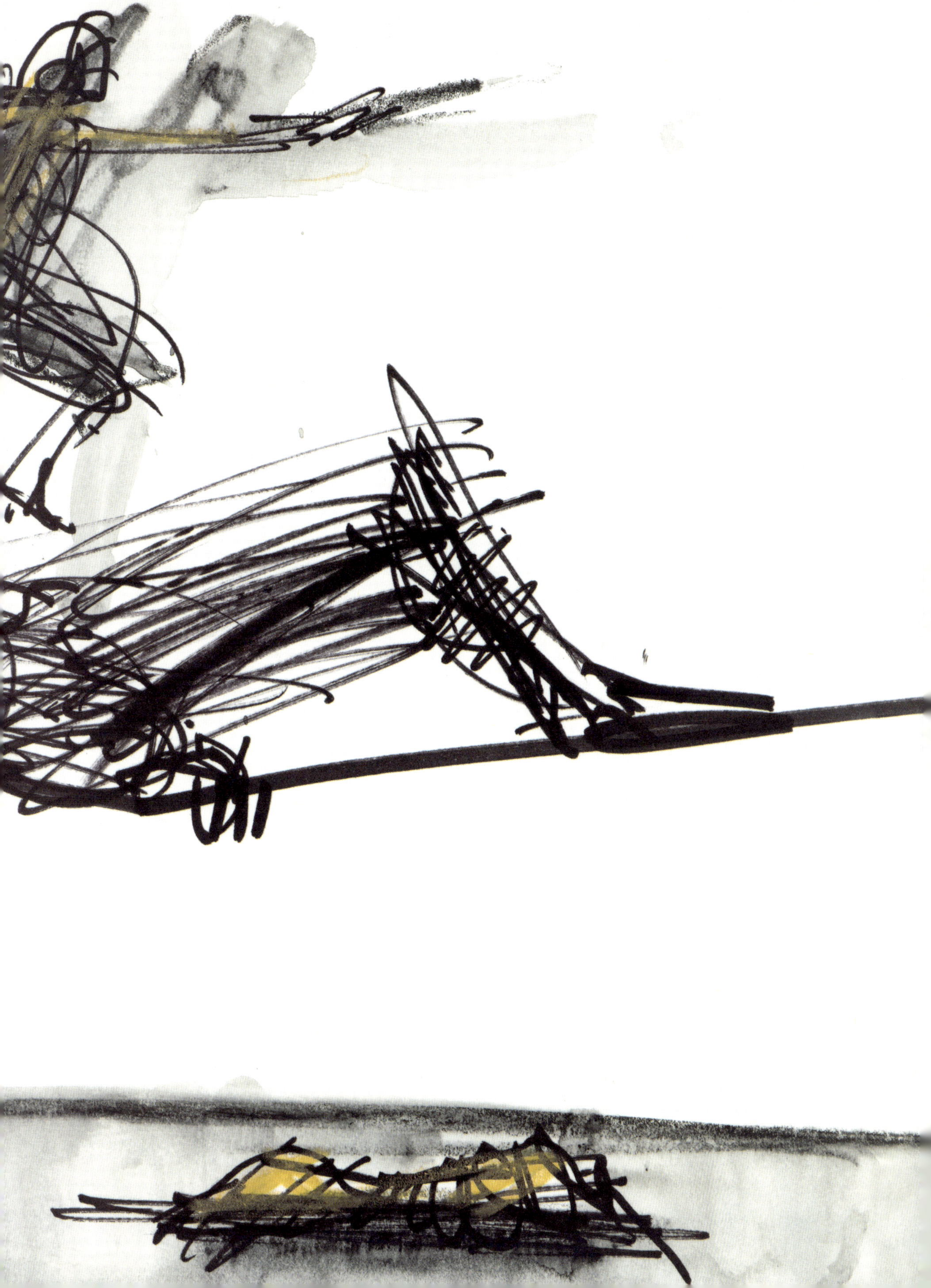

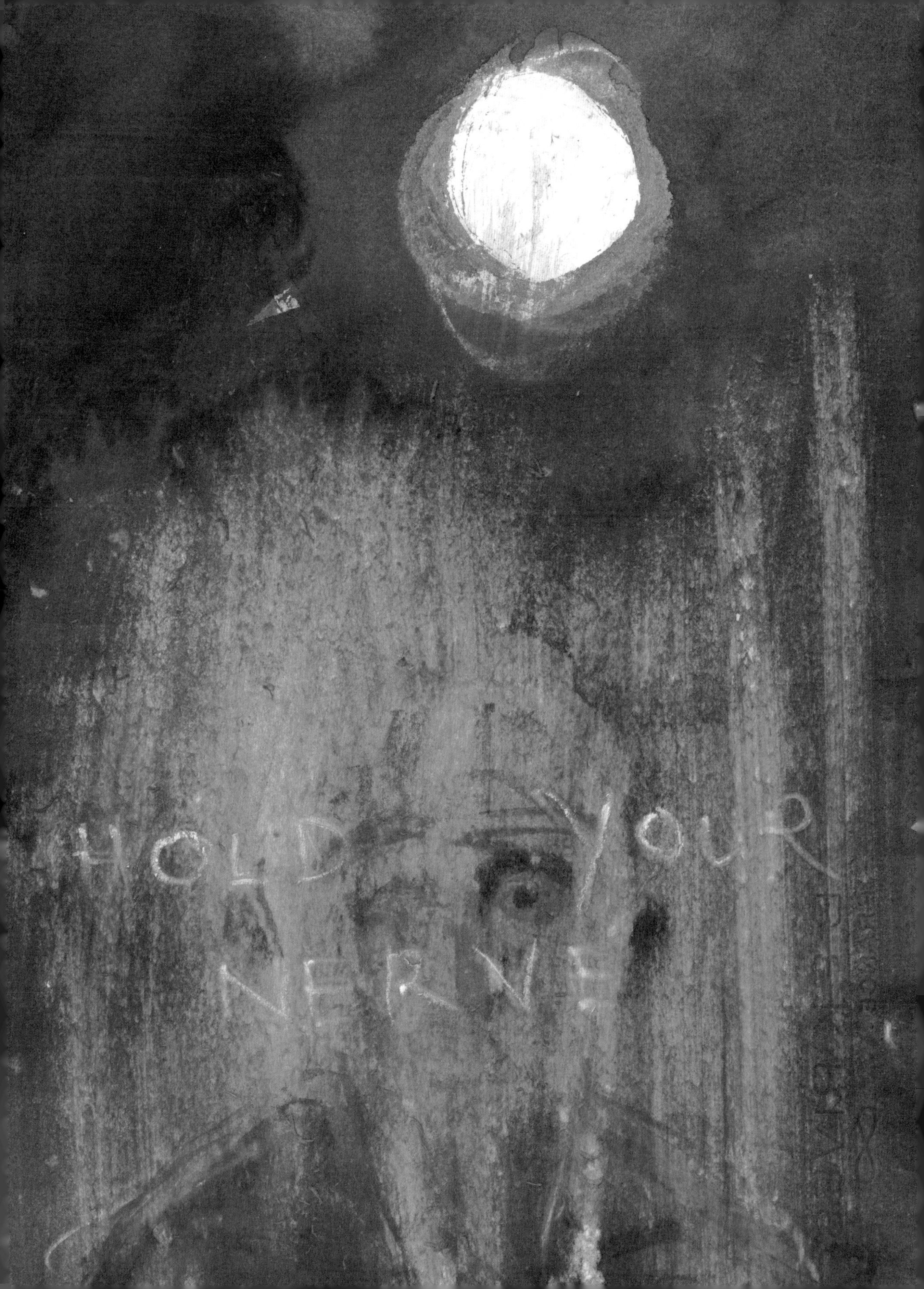
HOLD YOUR
NERVE

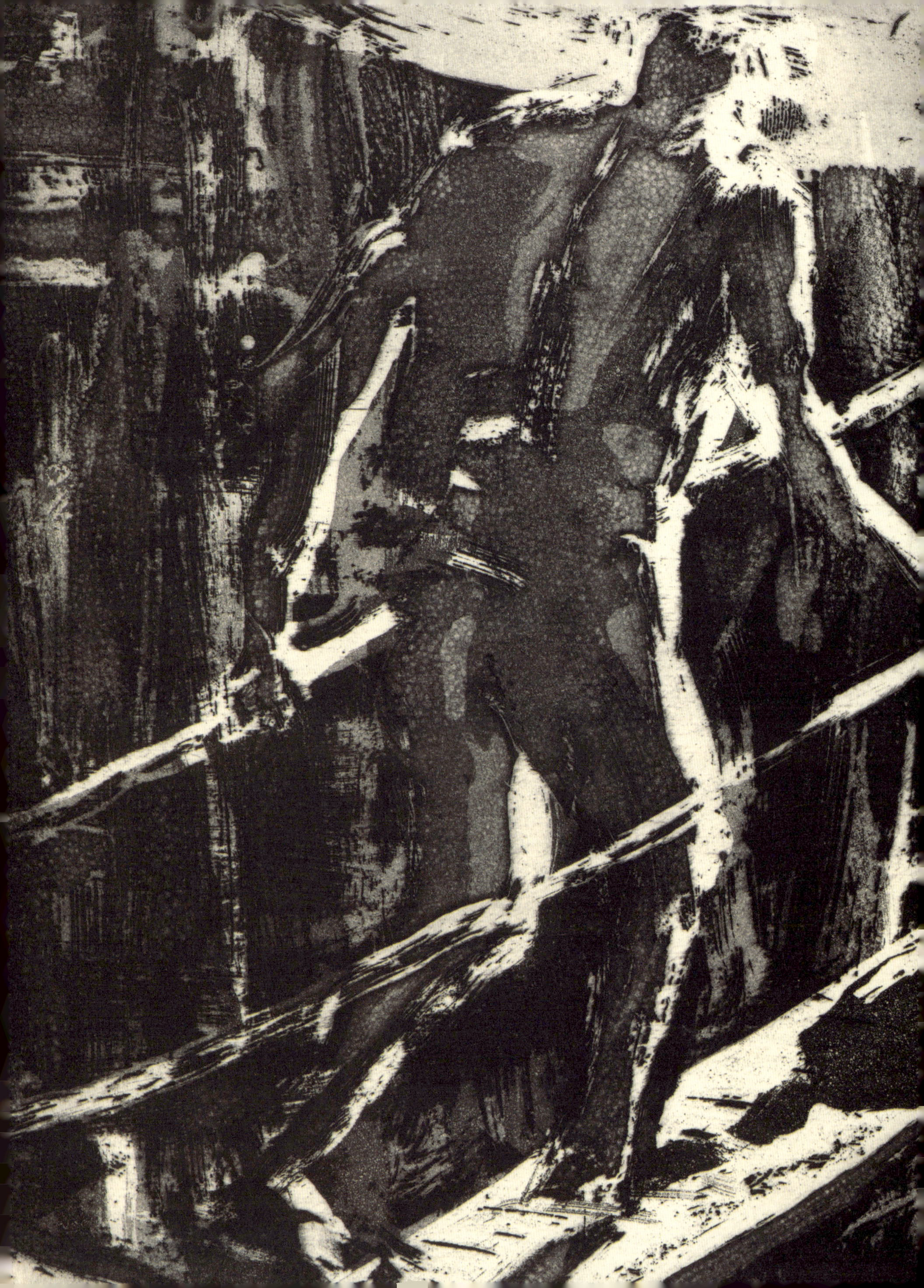

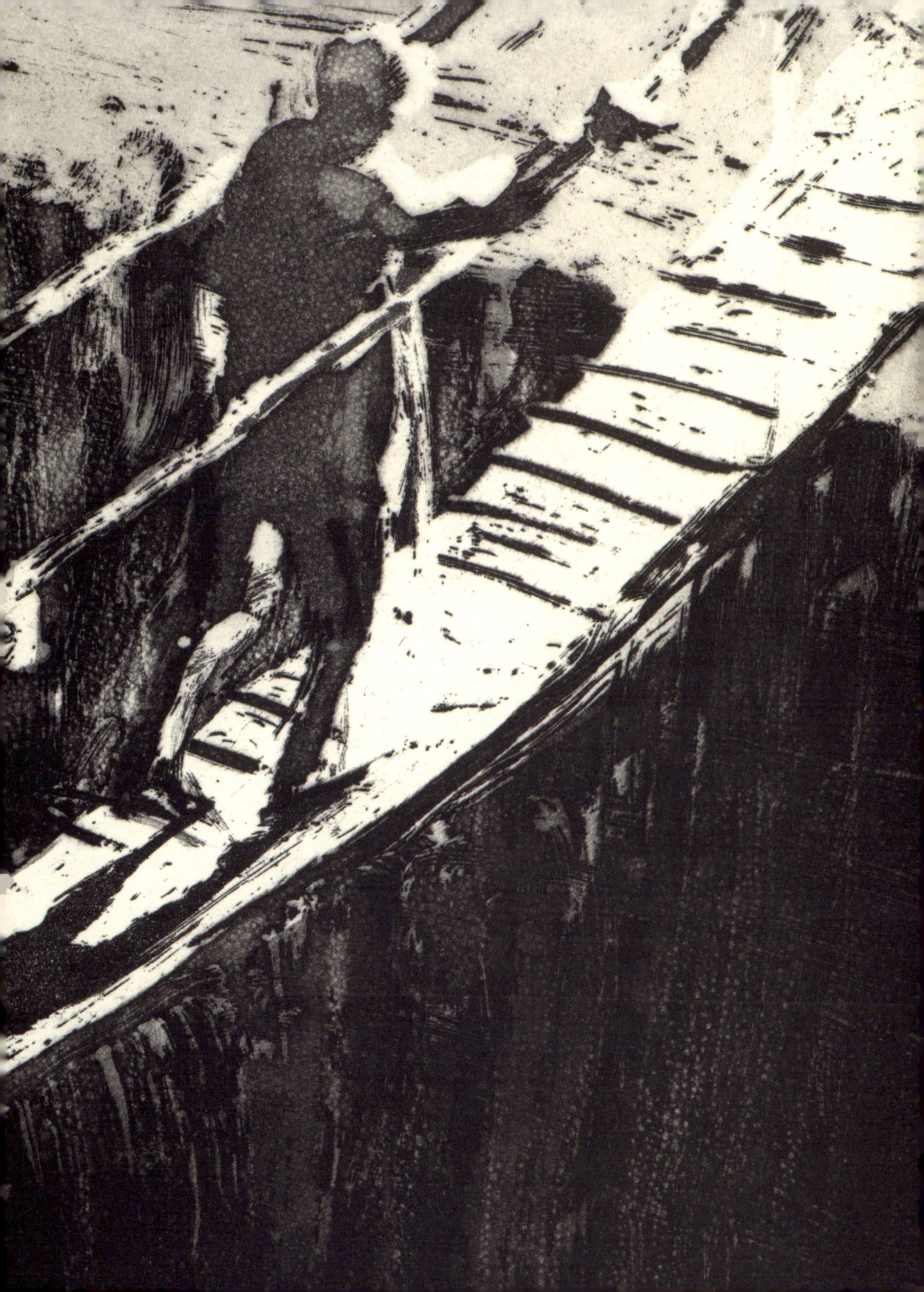

Years ago, I couldn't wait to get off the Brooklyn Bridge — the noise of the traffic was horrible. I considered turning back. But, to turn back seemed to go against the grain of engineered certainty. This hesitation lasted only for a few seconds before a wave of skaters and blade runners and joggers and women in power-walking sneakers turned me around and swept me on.

I came down the other side, and the noise was still horrible. And so I felt let down by that bridge. Nothing had changed.

It didn't compare with the excitement of the bridge from childhood. I was where I shouldn't be — because when I looked down, I saw others still bound to the earth. I could see them as they could not see themselves. I could see their distant pinheads as they checked their letterboxes or got in and out of cars. The ant colony in full display. It occurred to me that I, too, was an ant, but could I be? Because look at where I happened to be. I had got away, and if I had got away then what did that make me? A fugitive ant? But no crime had been committed — just a brief parting, an exempting from the joint purpose of the life below.

I walked on, one steadying hand on the balustrade now, as another space opened up before me, a space where art is made.

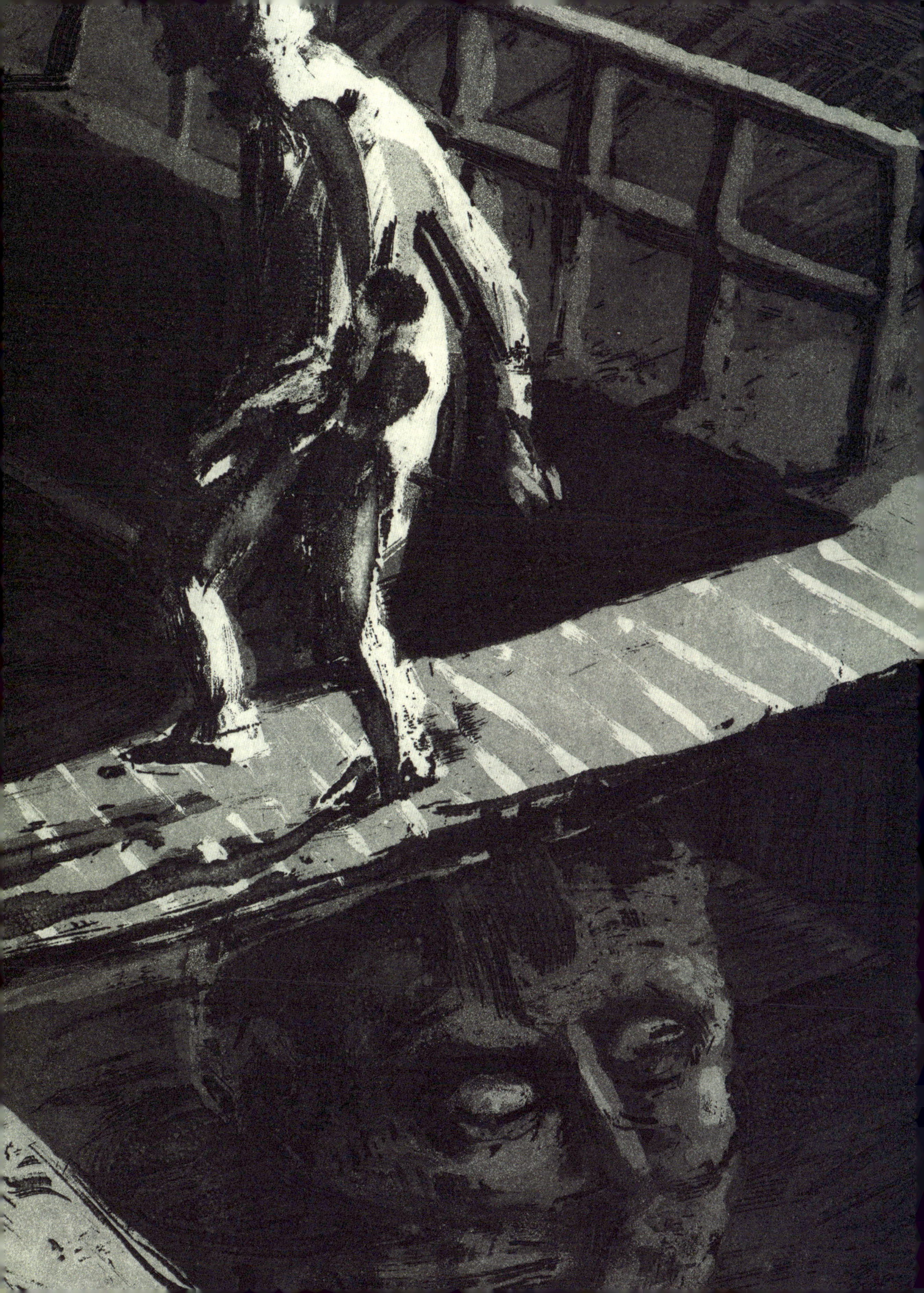

A darkening of skies, some red streaks as well, that distant afternoon when I came to a gathering of bridge builders who like to meet at sunset to watch the starlings dart and flock. Everything about the birds defies the rules the bridge builders adhere to — they weave a certainty out of wilfulness and randomness. Birds have no need of bridges, and it is this lack of dependency that makes the bridge builders a bit grumpy and their faces argumentative. Theirs is a private discipline. They are magicians, but without the capes or roll of drums. From their tightly squeezed eyes spill numbers and calculations. They make jokes no one else can understand, and when the joke ends in sniggering . . . a thought flies off to the old timbered bridge quaking under its modern weight.

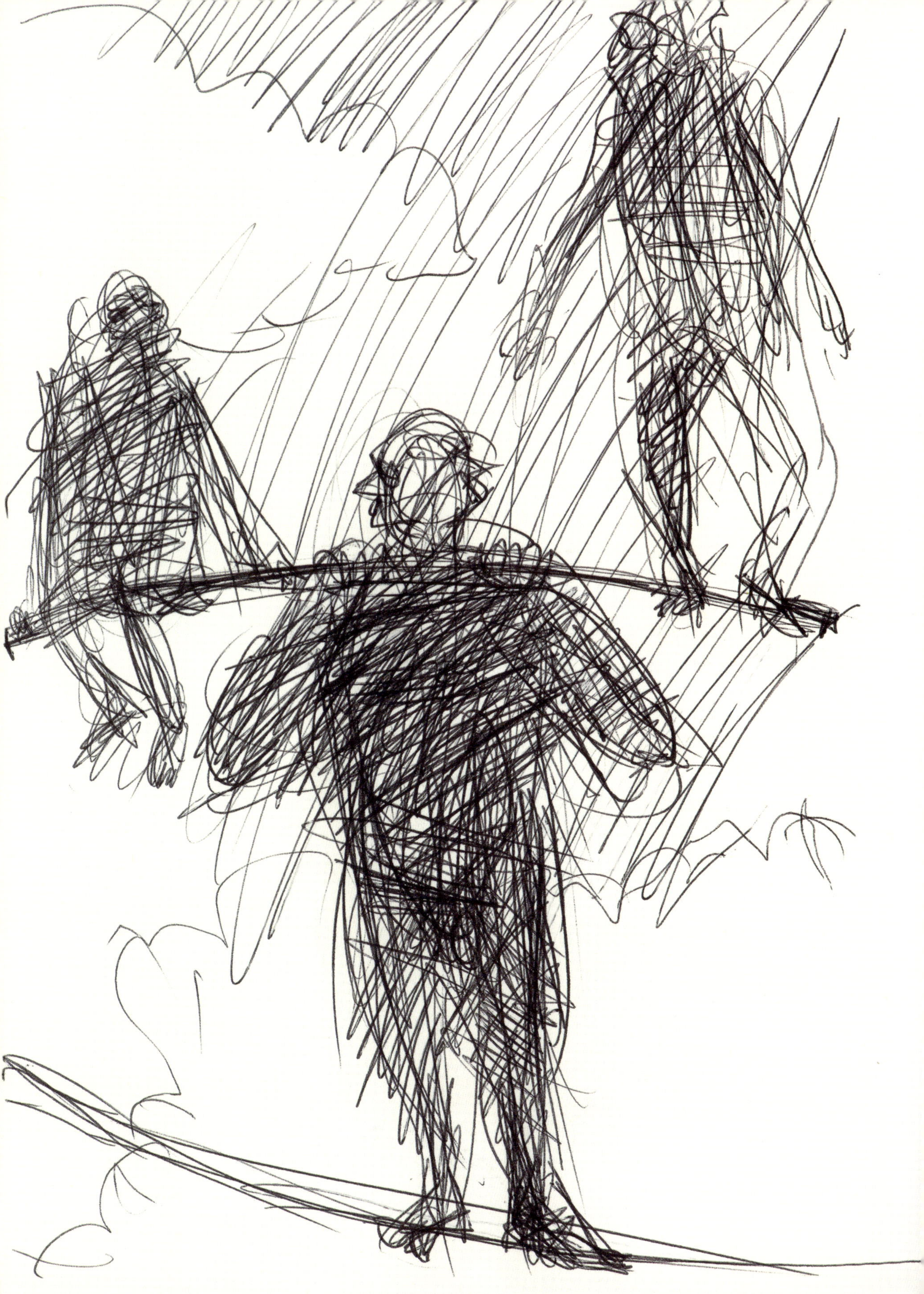

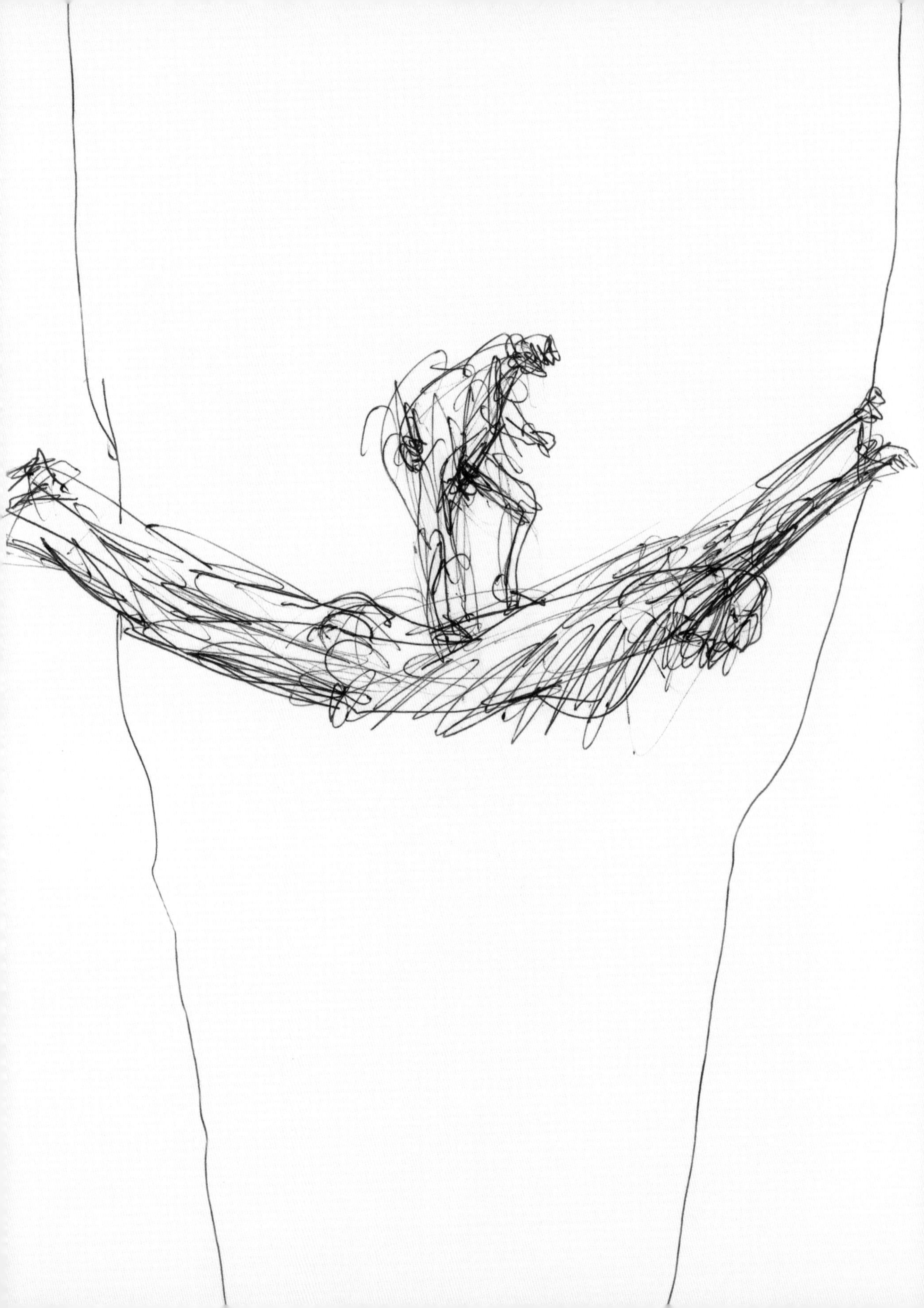

It is the saddest bridge in the world.

Think of two people stranded indefinitely at either end of the bridge, unable to close the gap, and left to gaze at one another.

Theirs is the bridge to nowhere. It leaves the far bank, broaches the river, then plunges headlong into thick hillside bush. It didn't work. He/she never listened to me. Words that explain the end of the affair also speak for the mute state of the bridge to nowhere. One half of the endeavour sincere to the very end. Blathering towards an assumed outcome. A gang of workmen up to their knees and thighs in the cold river. Their complaints unheard – filed away with the sprains and back spasms and pulled muscles of those who built the pyramids and Suez Canal.

Bridges are ruses. They play to our vanities. Here, this is just for you. Rise, dear friend. Rise and follow me across to where everything will be better forever after.

Neil Armstrong looked up one night and began floating to the moon.

The bridge Einstein started across wasn't even finished. He had to construct it as he went.

Usain Bolt ran and leapt; others were left on the far bank, wondering how he got there. Bill Gates imagined a world of invisible bridges where a man in Nigeria and a woman in Inverness would throw their hands up in horror at the very same moment as a man tumbled over Niagara Falls in a wine barrel.

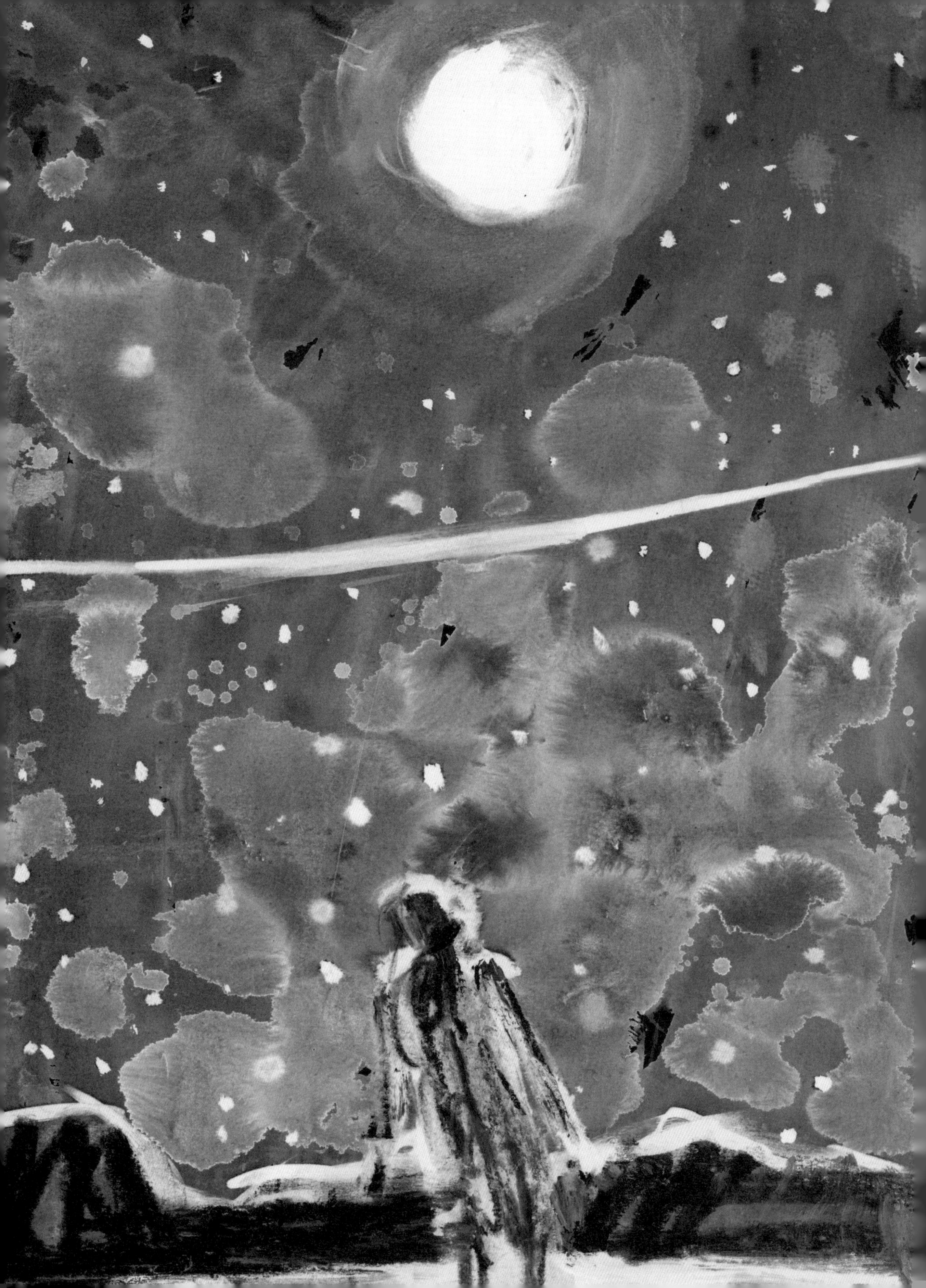

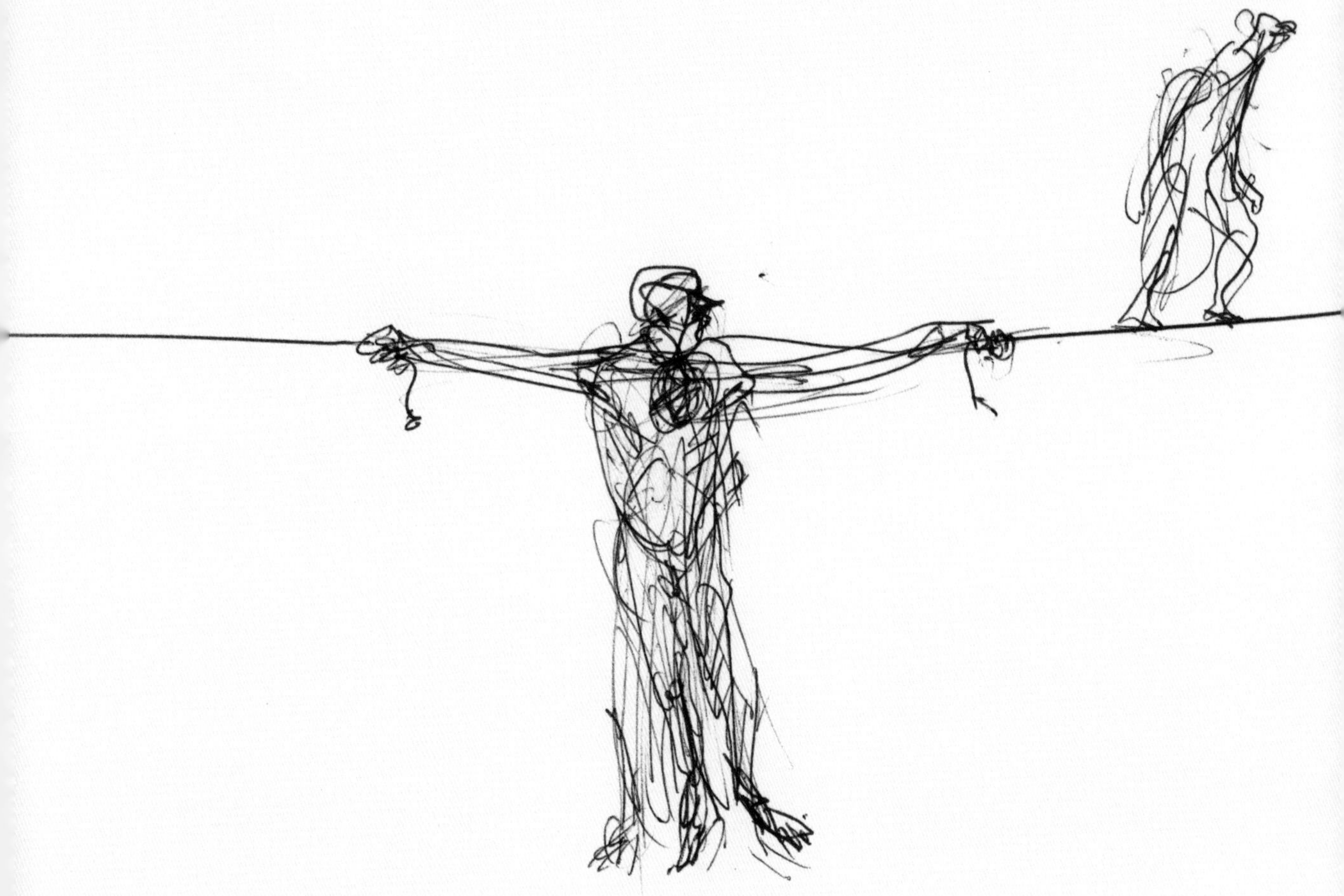

Once upon a time there was here and over there — natural, independent states until a bridge decided otherwise.

The ancestry of the bridge begins with the leaping shadow of a spooked fish. The grace of a tree limb lowering and spreading across a fast-moving creek may also have played its part.

But, of course, first the dinosaurs have to be seen off, then a brief wait for Homo sapiens to rise to their feet — for flight and escape and desire to transform the landscape.
The first bridge is built, and the word 'transcendence' has to be invented. Because where the first tremulous bridge builder now stands is not on land, nor in the water, nor in the air.

I often think about what the world would look like if it were to abandon its bridges. Longing would return to the landscape. The girl would be over there. She would remain forever after over there. Poems would need to be written to bring her into focus.

Before there were bridges, parts of the world were kept secret. Distance and various obstacles had to be identified and named — mountains and oceans. As soon as they were named, they became known and fell under human hegemony. And half a second later the question arose: what are they concealing? What do they hold behind themselves?

This growing ambition of ours made us intemperate. We began to think, why not make that island over there ours? A bridge must be built out to it. Well, soon after that was achieved, the island was no longer alone. It was joined to us. A sapling was carried across and planted. A pail of water was delivered. And the palm grew. The bridge was swept away in a typhoon. Now the ravaged palm gazes from its lonely aspect across the sea. Whenever it identifies the distant and waving mops of leaves, it knows instantly where it has come from, and begins to dream its ancestral story of a bridge.

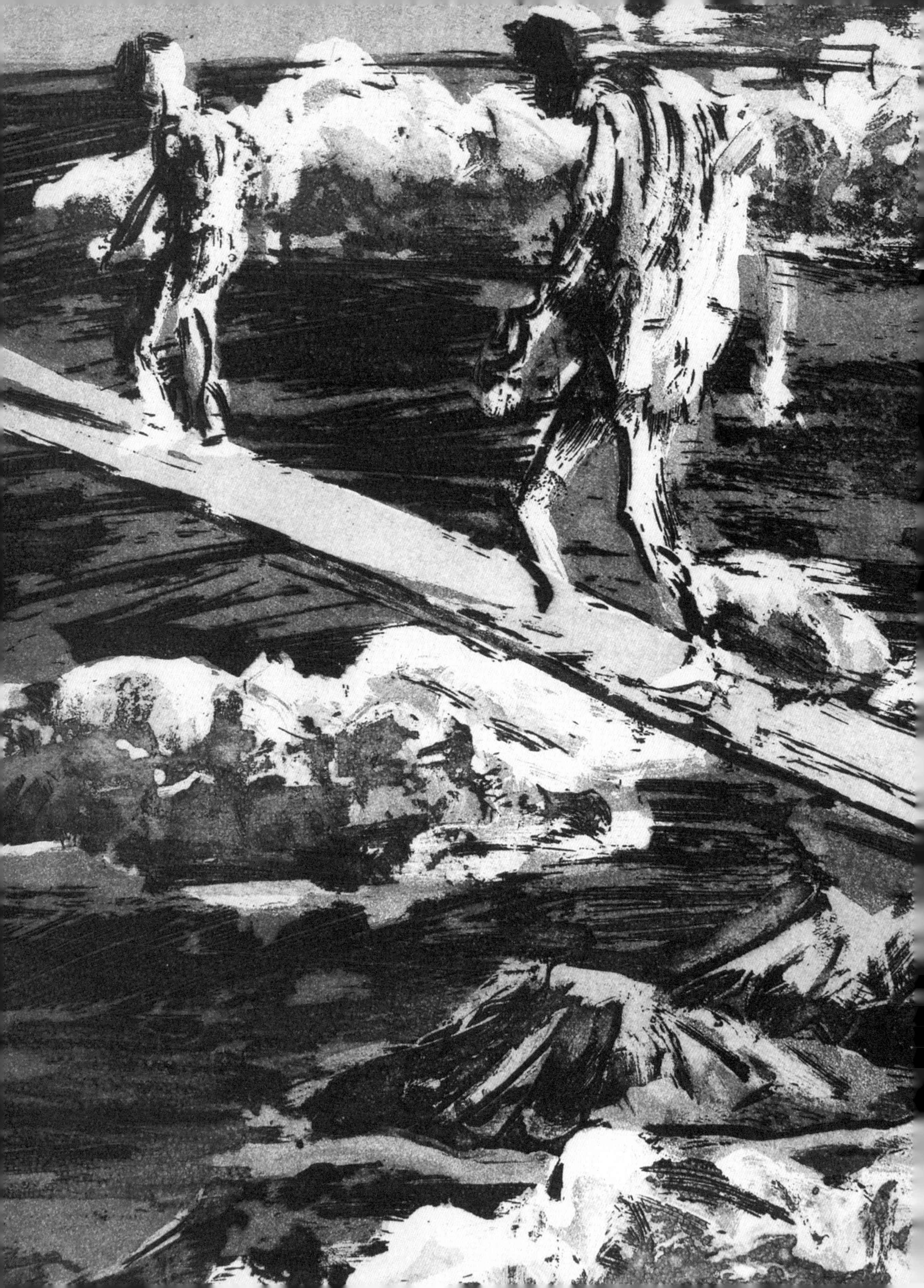

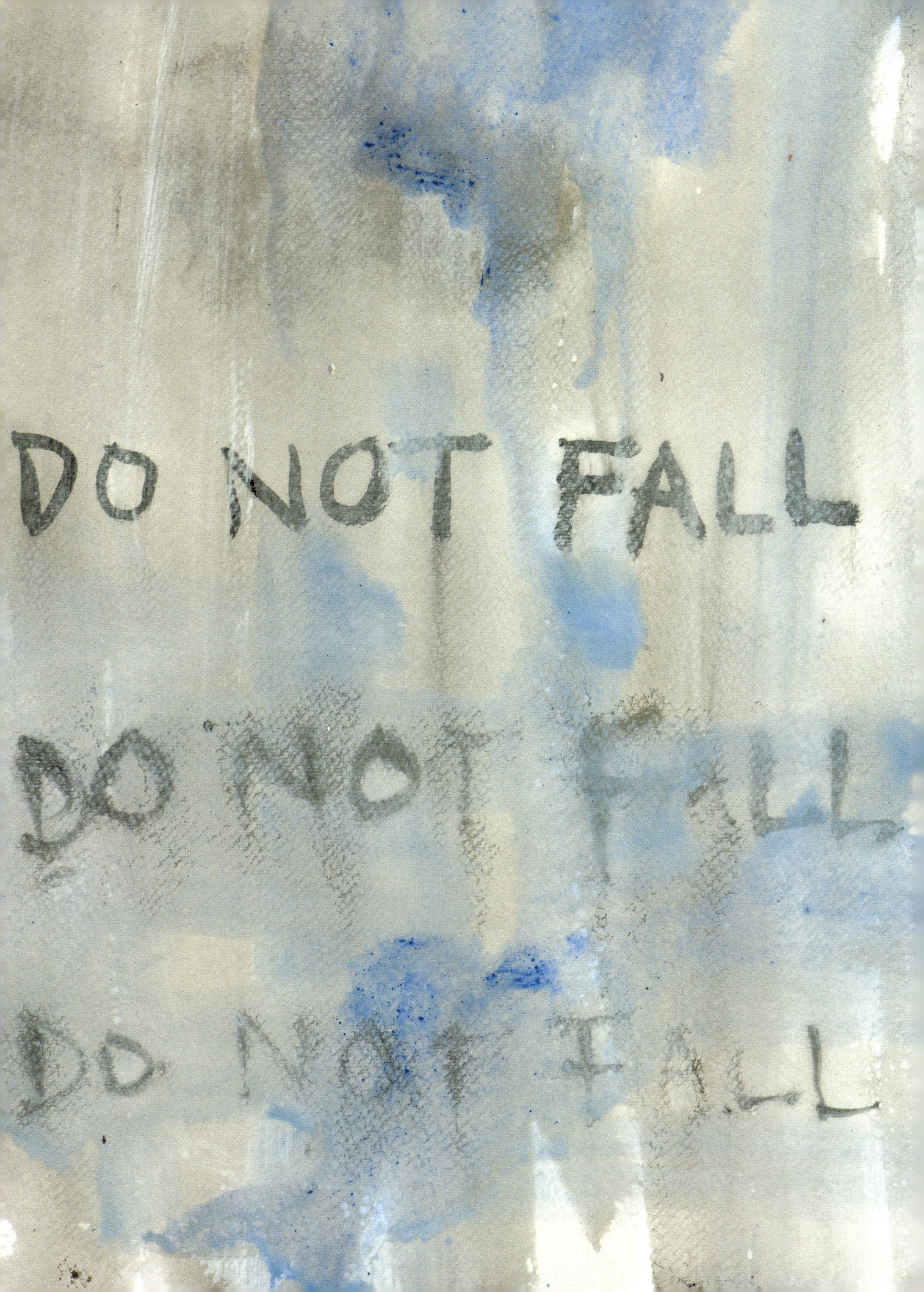
DO NOT FALL
DO NOT FALL
DO NOT FALL

Over that winter that Macleod and I wrote to each other I had the strongest sense that he was drawing his way towards me — back to his homeland, and birthplace. The shoulders of the figures sloped peacefully forward — at times purposeful, at other moments haggard in their deportment, and I wondered if in idle moments, slumped in his hammock at the back of his house off Parramatta Road, in Sydney, he had summoned me on my own bridge-building, a lone and spectral figure leaning into his work and paving his own way with words.

This brush stroke, and that very deliberate one. The struts and wires of his imagination.

What is it to paint your way back — or across?

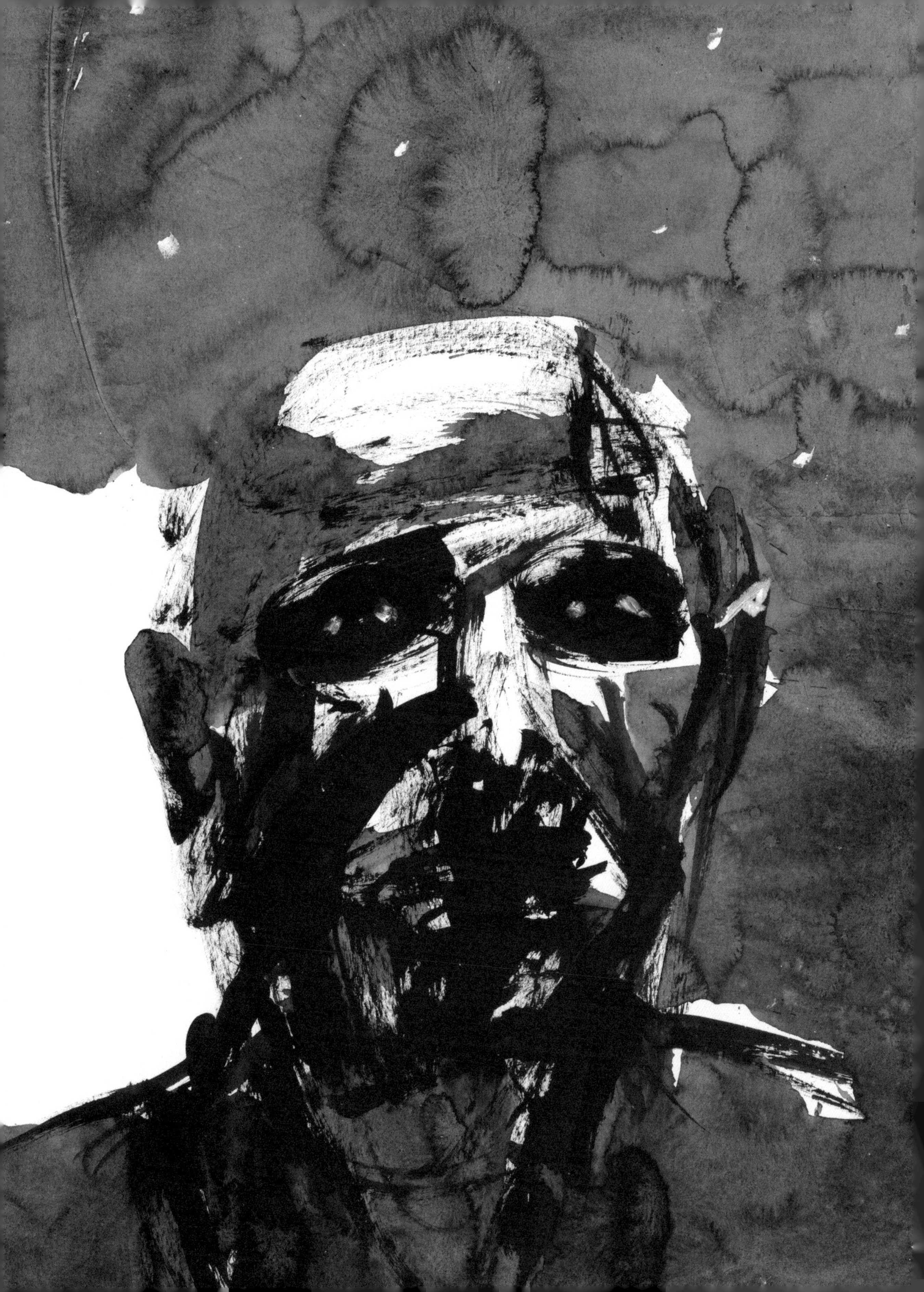

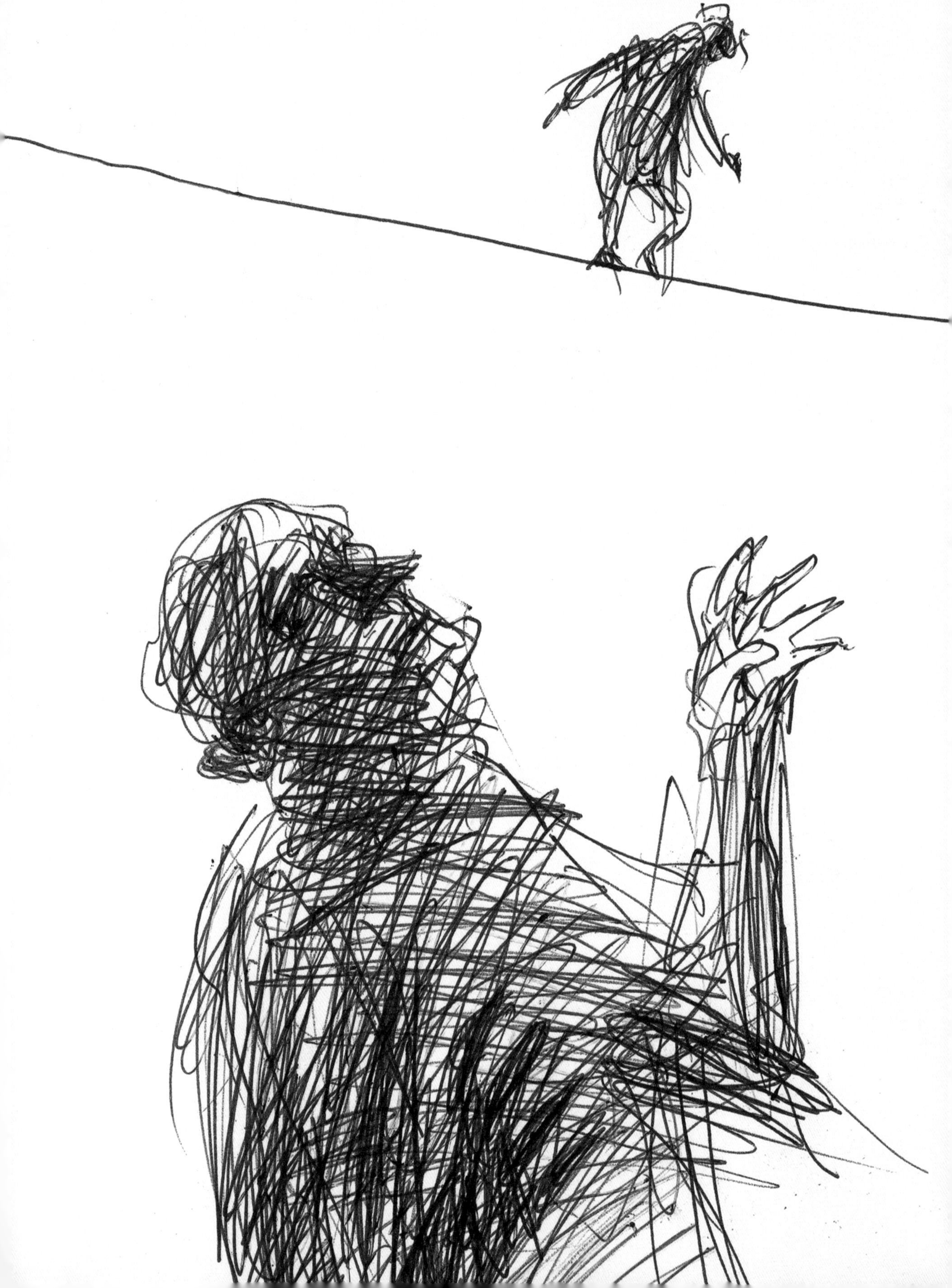

High above the afternoon gloom of Glenmore Street, and already halfway across the viaduct, I stopped as if hit over the head by a memory of Macleod's punching bag hanging from his studio ceiling near his canvases. The depressions in the bag caused by Macleod's kicks and punches. A splatter of paint on the floor and on an easel. The studio filled with intentions, and with sudden explosiveness. And, in between, a dreaminess like a sea, like the Tasman. A dreamspace that over time acquires a concreteness. Like an empty cell conditioned to the pacing of its solitary prisoner. Because that is where I thought Macleod had arrived — the artist, and others, hundreds, probably thousands of the handful known to me, who had made the trip across in the nineteen eighties. Setting out, setting across, with their hopes and lightly packed suitcases. The bridge widening and spreading with an ease that must have surprised many in those days. That generation married, put down roots in Sydney's eastern beaches; their kids grew up without a thought for the place that their parents escaped to each night in their sleep.

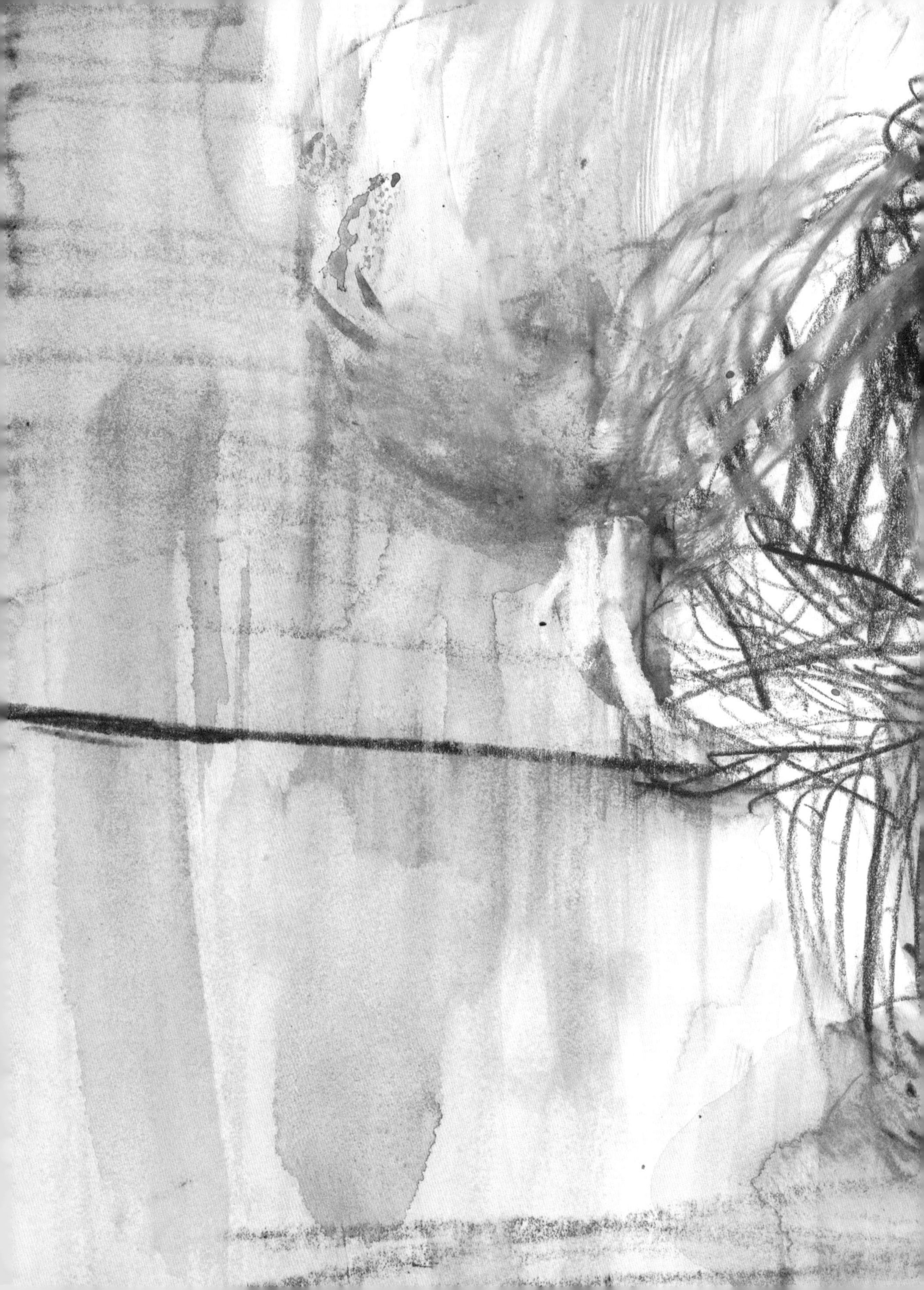

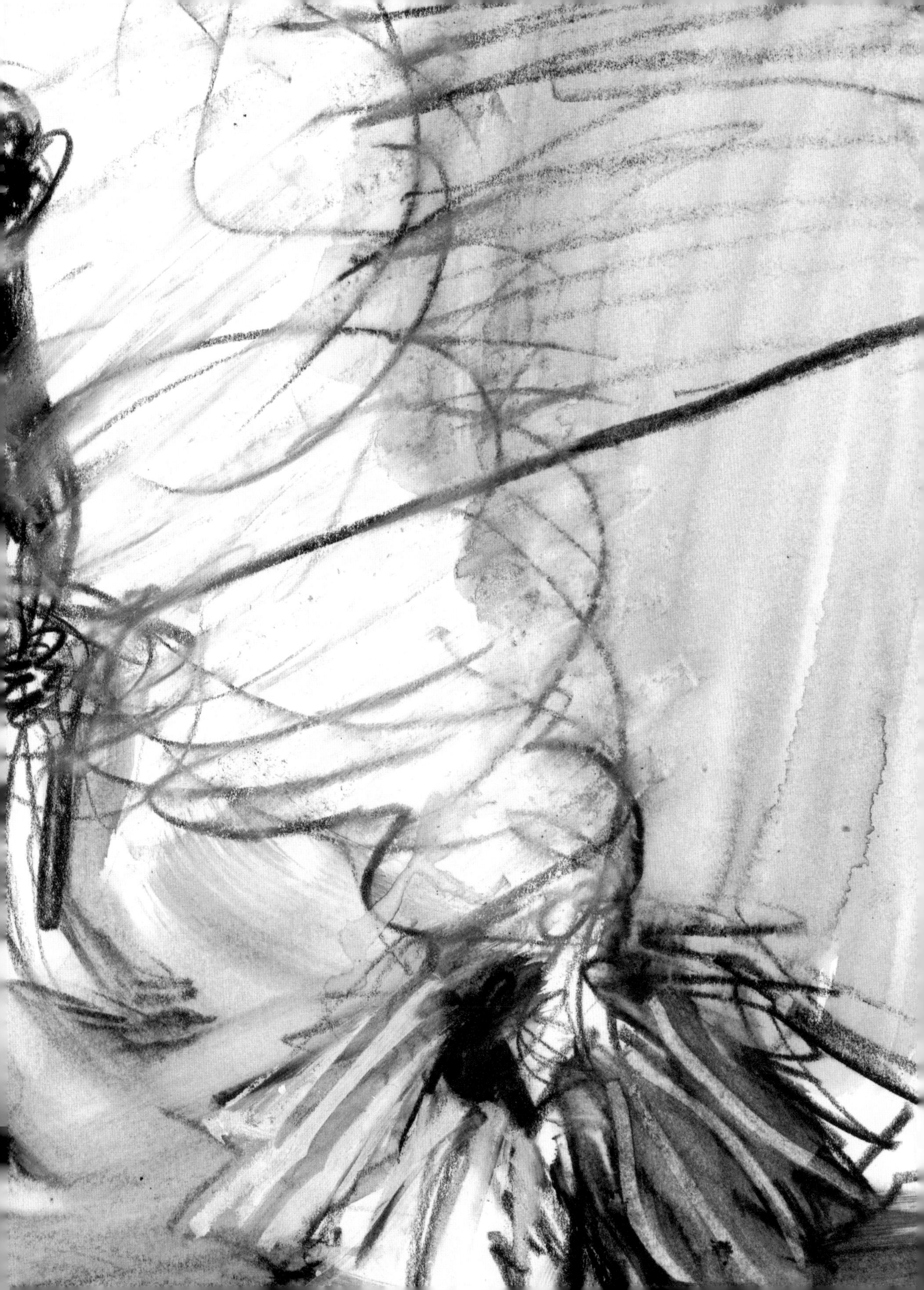

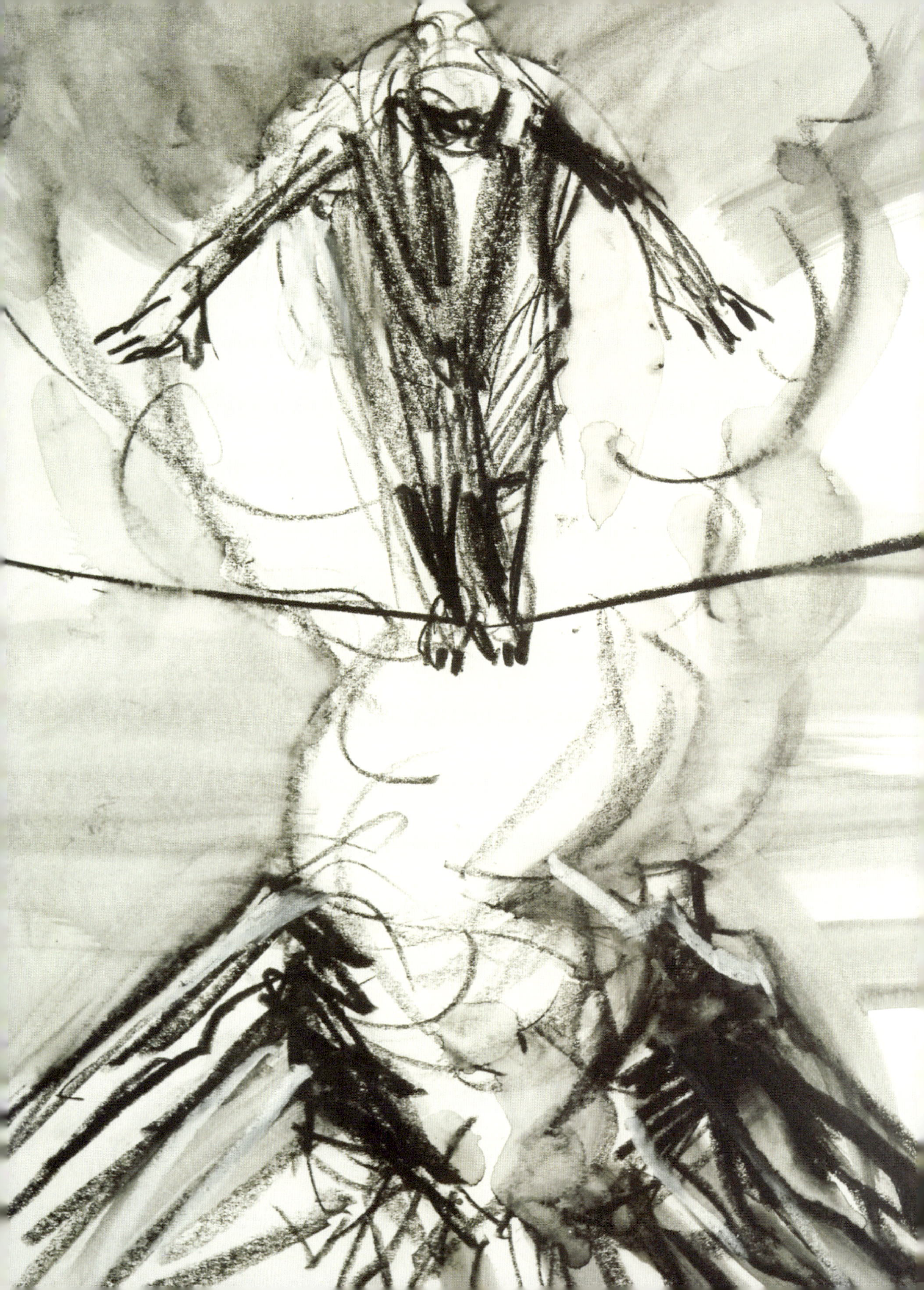

The grey green of here
The fertilised green of there
The rocking ocean in between
Macleod in his hammock

The giant red spans launch themselves into the blue Tasman sky. Then, what? It is like any other bridge. You step forward, and before it has even landed you are already beginning to rise. I took another step, then another; I hurried the next dozen steps until the ground below parted and spread in all directions. And I was lifted into a space unclaimed by language. A needling thrill that started at the back of my neck and travelled directly to my testicles whenever I drifted near the side. The scattered tin roofs of the coastal neighbourhood turned into clinging barnacles. I was enjoying the same view as a seagull with its tucked eye. Down there, from up here. The pack continued to weigh heavily on my shoulders as packs do over the first hour of any journey. Soon the struggle between shoulder bone and strap was over, and I was able to concentrate on the view.

A wriggling line of white spittle tracked the edge of the dark coastal hills where Wellington plunges into Cook Strait. No wonder the first arriving fishermen from Stromboli thought they had gone full circle and arrived back at their volcanic island when they looked up at the brooding and unfriendly hills tossed up at the backs of the surging waves.

The same sea unfurling itself onto the fine sand of Bondi pounds the rocky edge of Wellington's south coast. A bridge must ignore that kind of local circumstance. The task of a bridge is to grasp two possibilities without favour. One is either coming or going. Much like a tide, I suppose — the motion or at least the possibility of conveyance being of greater interest to it. And although it may not state it so explicitly, either in life or fairy tales, a bridge offers the same promise as the pot of gold at the end of the rainbow. Far below, the choppy sea turned distant and flat. To the east, the snow-capped peaks of the Kaikōuras. Ahead, the soaring red spans — encouraging and dazzling in the sunlit blue, then so swiftly buried in cloud that my heart almost disappeared with them.

I had to reel myself in and bring my concentration back to a single breath.

Now, to the south-east, lay a very new country, geologically speaking, with a bustling new conversation about how we are to live in its conditions and with one another. To the north-west an ancient country, with an ancient conversation barely audible or listened to.

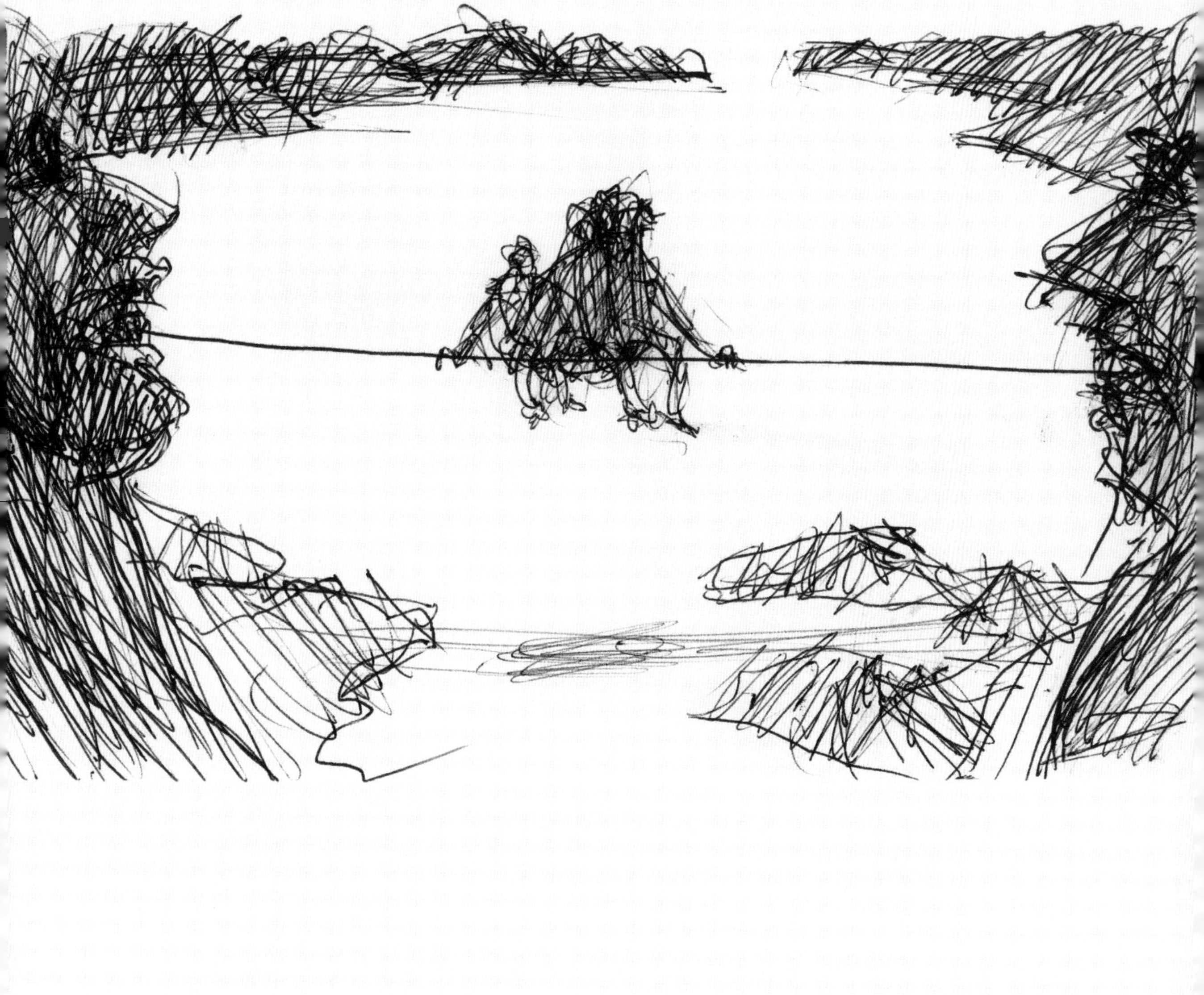

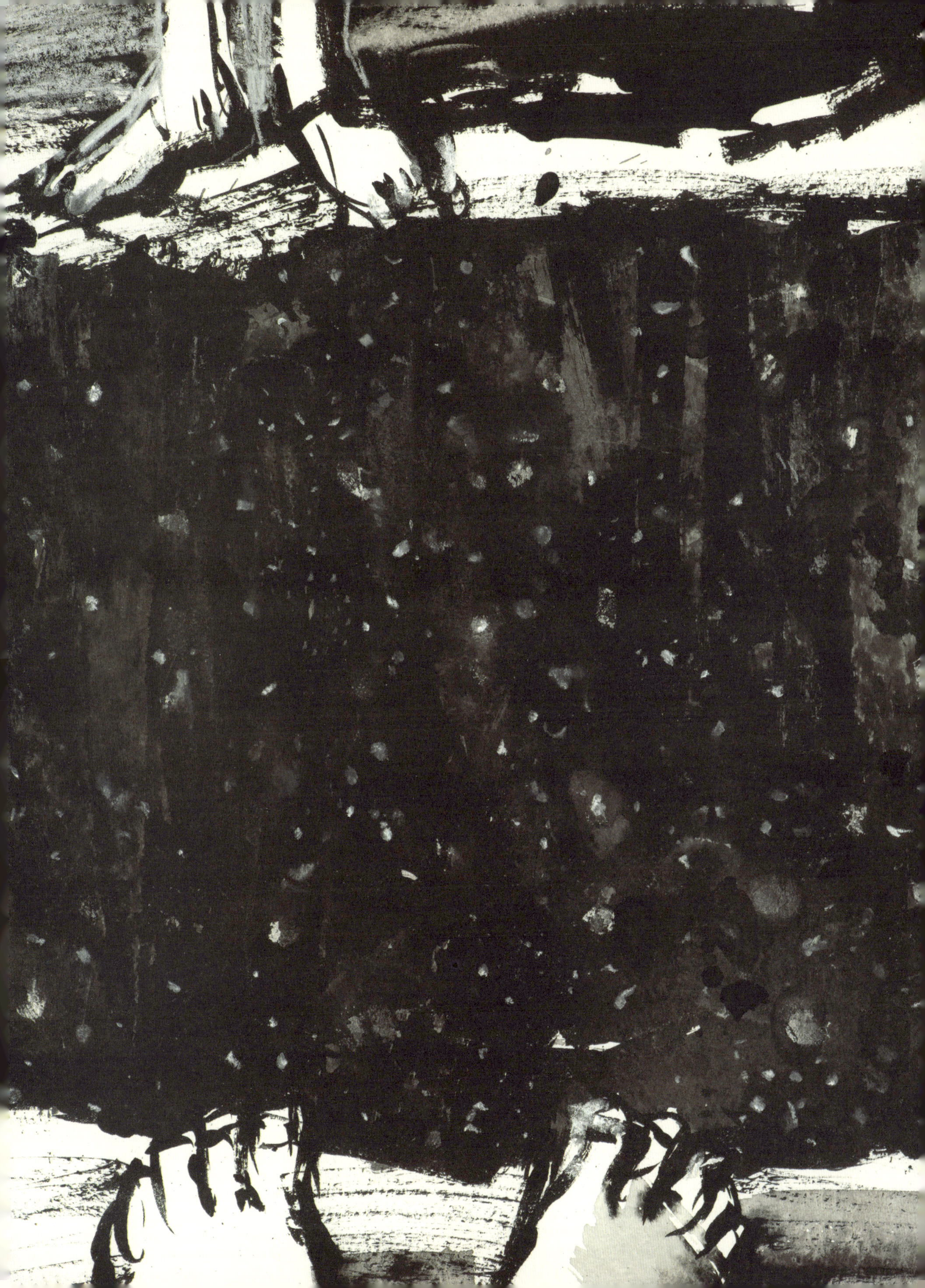

It is nerve-wracking to be the first — to be the first at anything. In time I imagine these footprints of mine will be trampled under by the trans-Tasman foot traffic.

Look at what has happened to the Hillary Step. Hikers with more money than sense breathing their ambition into the mouth of death parading itself as immortality. Joyless souls determined to land their puny footprints in those of giants.

The old joy returns. The lightness underfoot. Some soaring expectation let loose.

A span rose like a red orange thread into blue sky. I took a step, then another. The sea, at first so furious with my stunt, now flattened out to a regular blue pattern.

When the children were small, and we holidayed in Golden Bay, we loved the wide sandy bridges that disappeared on a change of tide — and in the time it took to bat an eyelid a fishing boat now gently puttered where a few hours ago we walked across the wet sand looking for a pipi bed to raid. That lovely fringe of sand in the shape of a bird's beak and with the beautifully melancholic name of Farewell Spit passed below. And, in an instant, the world turned blue. Blue above and below. And ahead, a glow of sun-rinsed blue.

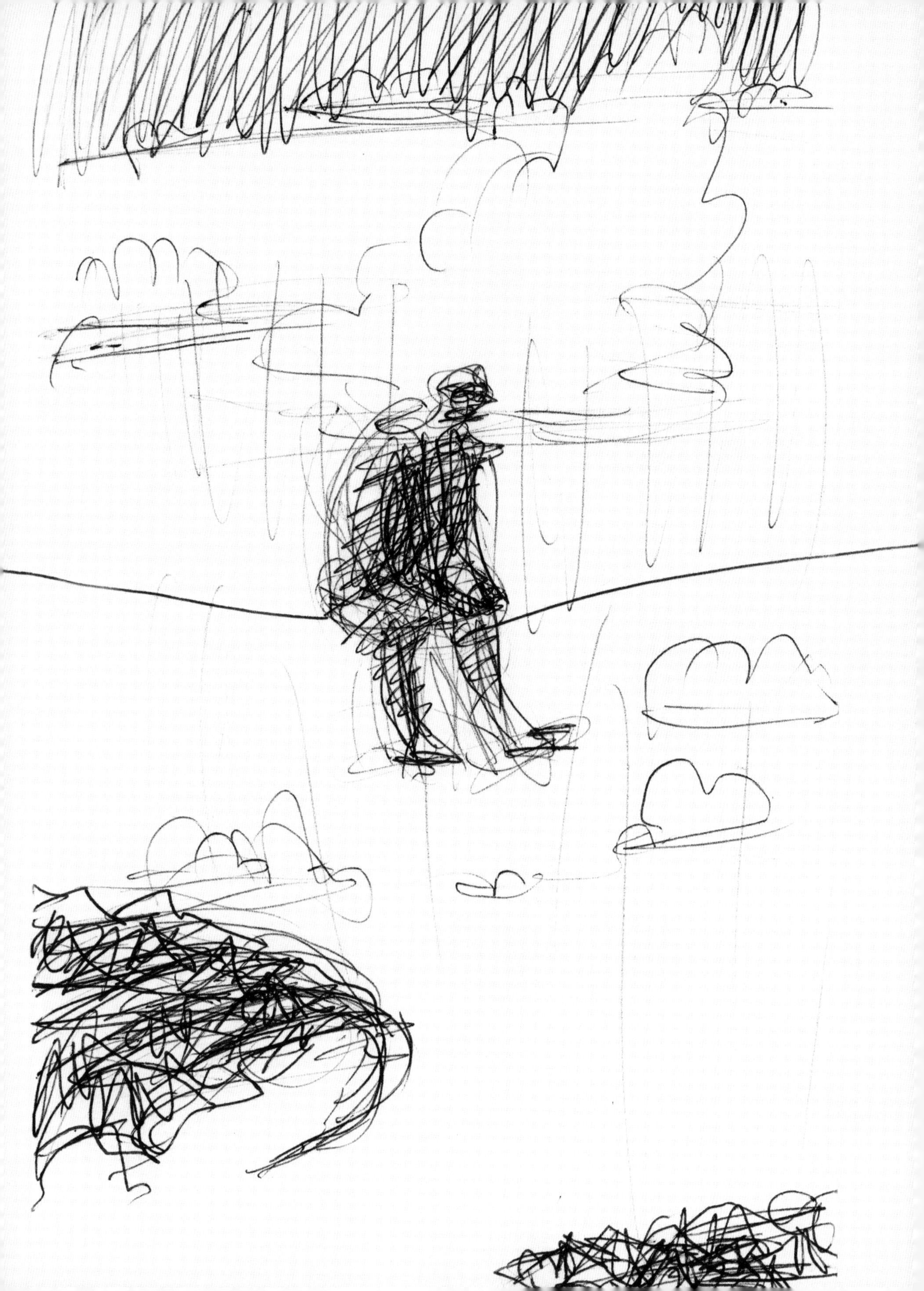

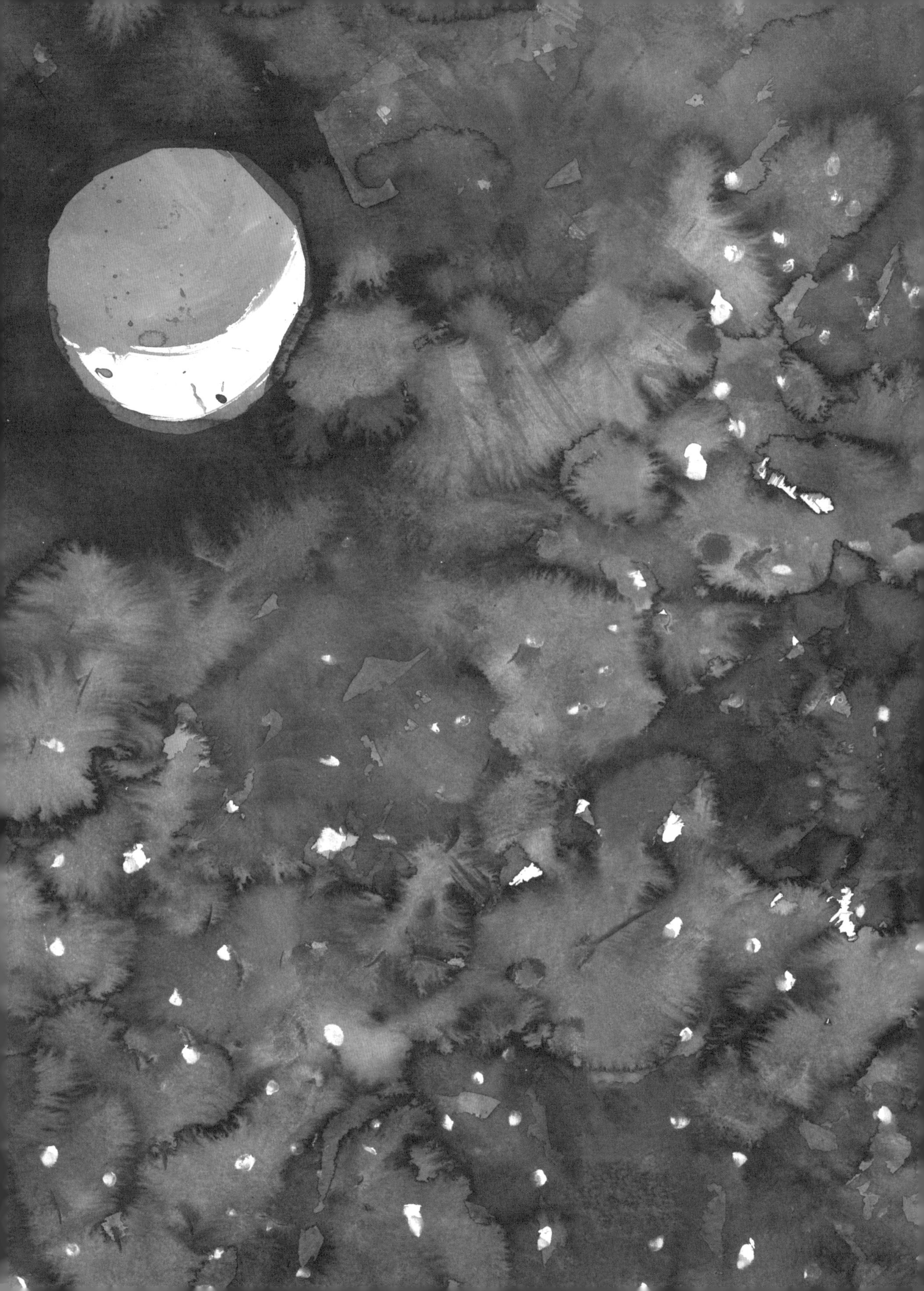

There are new proximities to think about. I don't recall the sun ever setting below me. But there it is shining upwards as it drags the cover of night after itself. I can no longer tell the sea or the sky apart. They enter through the same dark door which I cannot pass. I must keep on in the direction of the north star as it unfolds its welcome mat. And now the windows of the sky appear. Bright stars. And a moon that seeks out my company. The air is cold. But I am afraid to stop to pull on my coat and pull on my trackpants. I'm afraid that if I stop, I will fall out of the sky. If I stop, a sudden feeling of inertia will see my confidence sink under the weight of the night and the overwhelming scale of everything. I wish I could hear the waves. Just to have the company. I know the waves are down there. I know them as the stars know them. A dark wriggle in the lunar surface of the sea turns yellow as the cloud passes and the moon reappears. To the west, the steady light of an aeroplane on its direct and patient course.

A few years ago a kānuka seeded beneath the leaf drop of a very old hīnau. I saw a difficult future for them both, but couldn't bring myself to yank out the kānuka. Now, all these years later, they've learned to accommodate each other — one leans away from the other, like two people crossing a bridge.

I am more wary of people on a bridge than I am on a street.

Who can forget that moment the New York cop yells at Petit to get off the damn wire 'or else I'm gonna have to come out there and grab you'?

The unspoken thought we share as we prepare to pass by one another is the great height we're at — a moment ago it was exhilarating; now we're made aware of the threat of it, the lung-piercing drop below, how long it would take to fall.

We pass by, and those dangerous thoughts drift off with the fading footsteps of the other.

I must concentrate and not let go. I must not look down but stay focused.

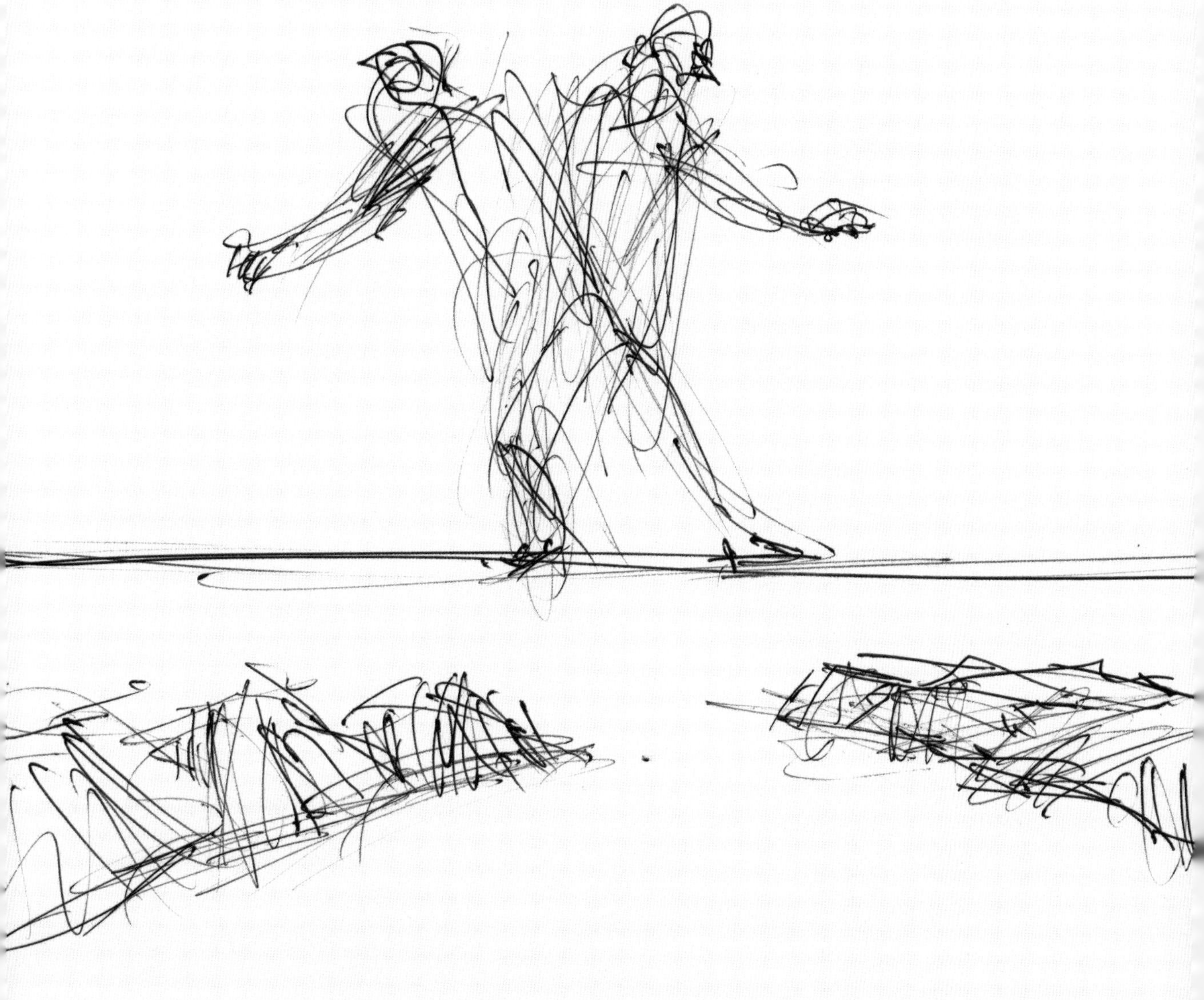

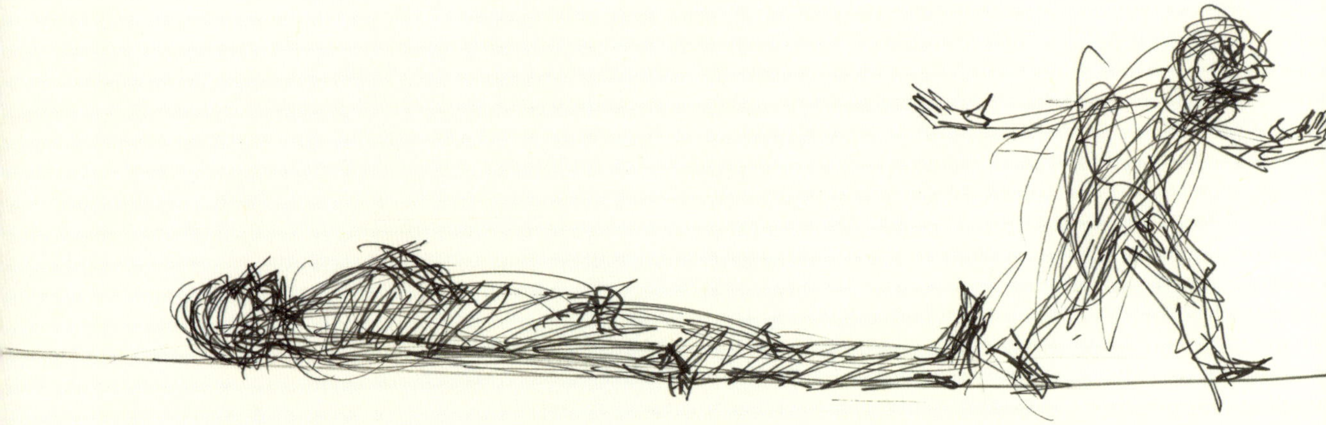

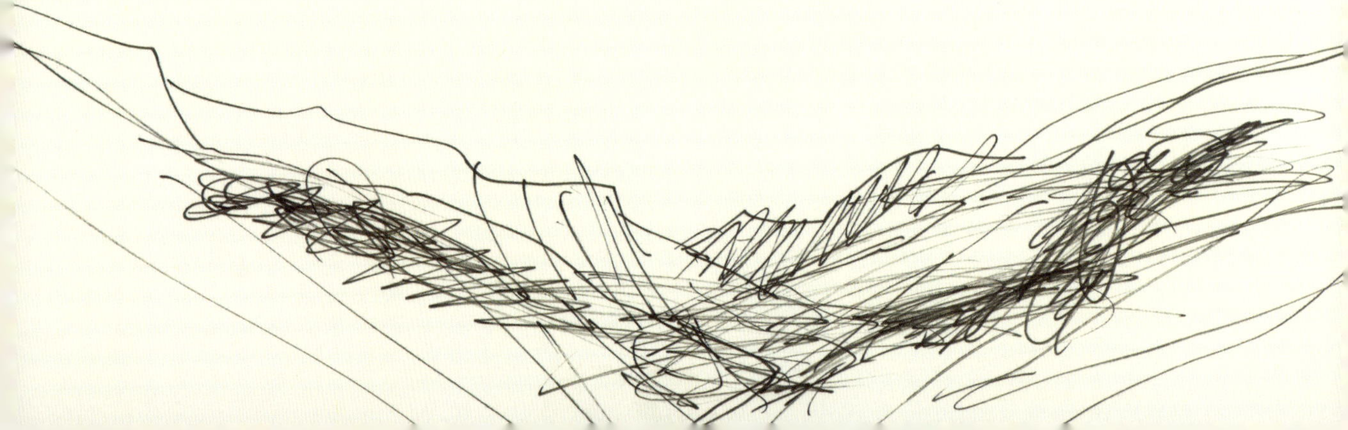

Once, in Kolkata, on a bridge over the Hooghly River, I encountered camps of people sleeping rough. Families lay side by side on sleeping mats, beneath the thin stalled legs of oxen, as cars beeped and bumped past. I had to step over and around their sleeping bodies. It felt unnatural, as though the bridge bore a weight that its engineering and construction had failed to take into account. The bridge lost some of its elegance, and some of its traditional usefulness was compromised.

I felt the same confusion of purpose when, years later, I witnessed some drunk fool successfully riding a sheep around a paddock.

In olden times, it's true, some people did live in small wooden accommodations set like miniature forts above bridges. Others were sent to rot in towers that also acted as entrances to bridges. These are exceptions. A bridge's core value is to deliver goods or people from one place to the other.

I woke to a shrill whistling in the cables, and I found myself cradled in a sunlit blue. The day had started without me. My heart missed a beat — but there it was, thank god, the day, where I had left it, cushioning the handrail. My calves ached. I had walked into the night for far longer than I had planned. I lit the primus, boiled some water for coffee, ate an unappealing muesli bar, attended to a few personal details — one I will mention, I brushed my teeth and spat over the side. At once the gesture turned puny as a gob of white spit disappeared within half a second of becoming atmospheric.
High above the Tasman I breathed in and filled my lungs. Back the way I'd come was a long fragment of thick cloud. In the other direction, the way forward climbed to a clear blue sky.

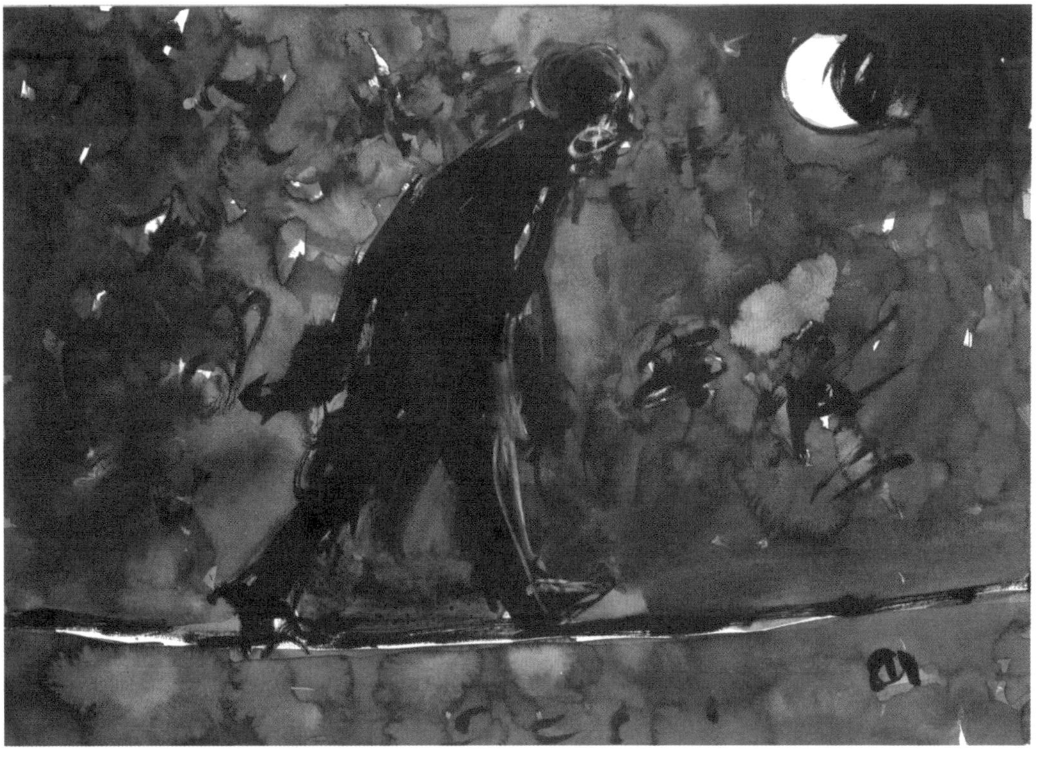

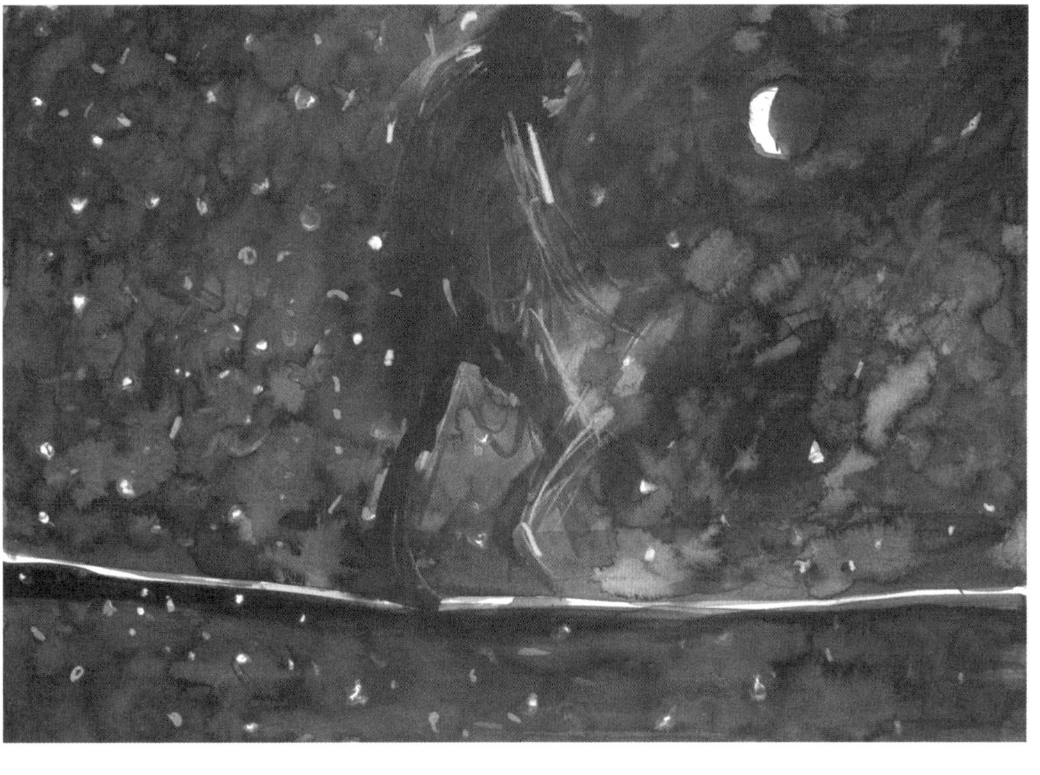

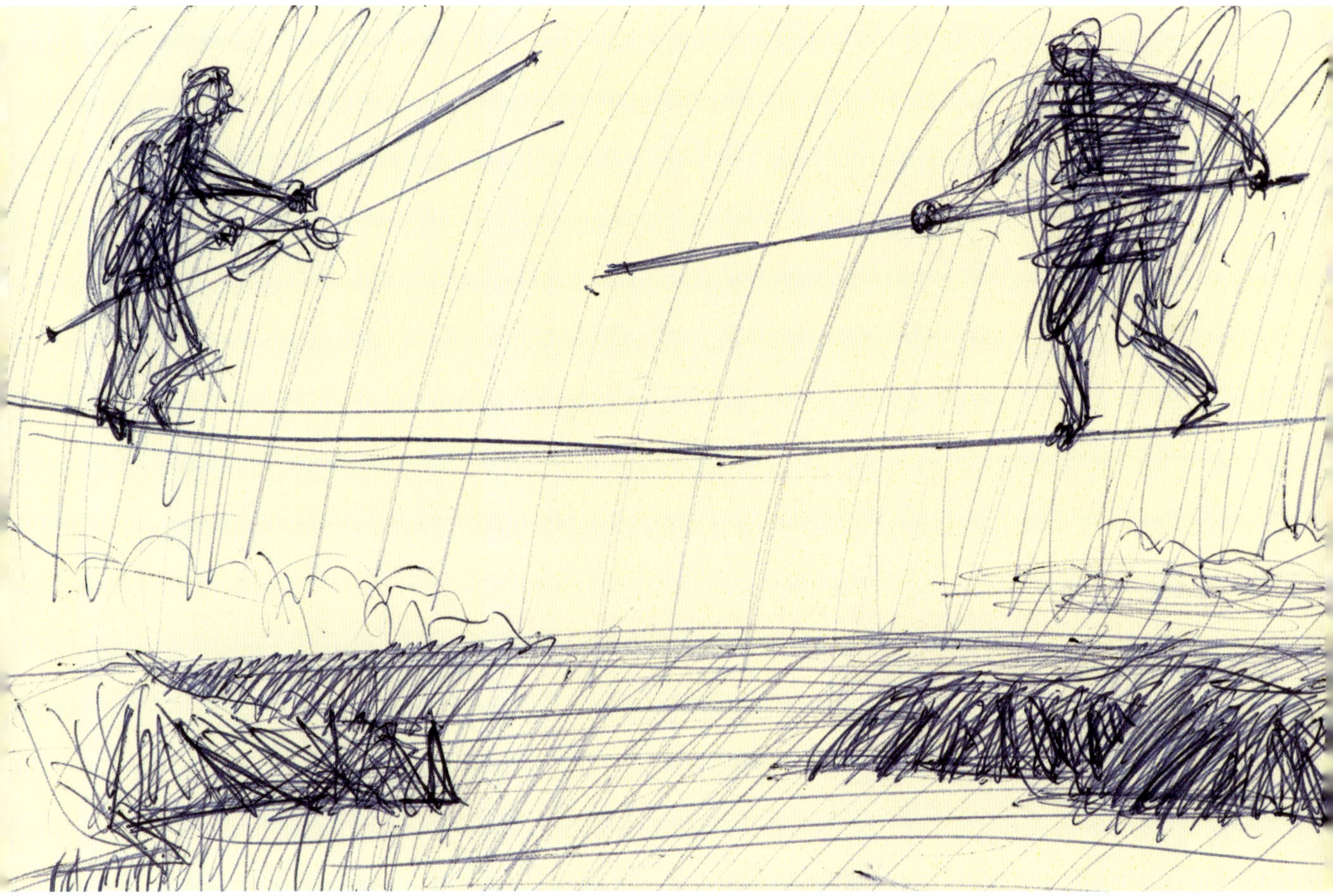

I pictured Macleod waking in his hammock, his homeward thoughts torn apart by the heckling of kookaburras. The two skies failing to merge as well as they do in his imagination. One cool and blowy, the other dusty and hot and filled with bird shrieks. The sun-drenched drawl of one place and the flat diphthongs of the other. The nuance of place jostling and pulling on the artist's elbow.

In the subconscious everything is up for grabs — there is no enforced geographical isolation. There are no trespass notices.

He is across the sea in a stride. There.

He's thought it, and so it exists, and this is how a kookaburra wakes him out of a dream located in the Port Hills of Lyttelton Harbour.

The trunk of the jacaranda and the hook in the door jamb would have nothing in common either, but for the arrangement of the hammock.

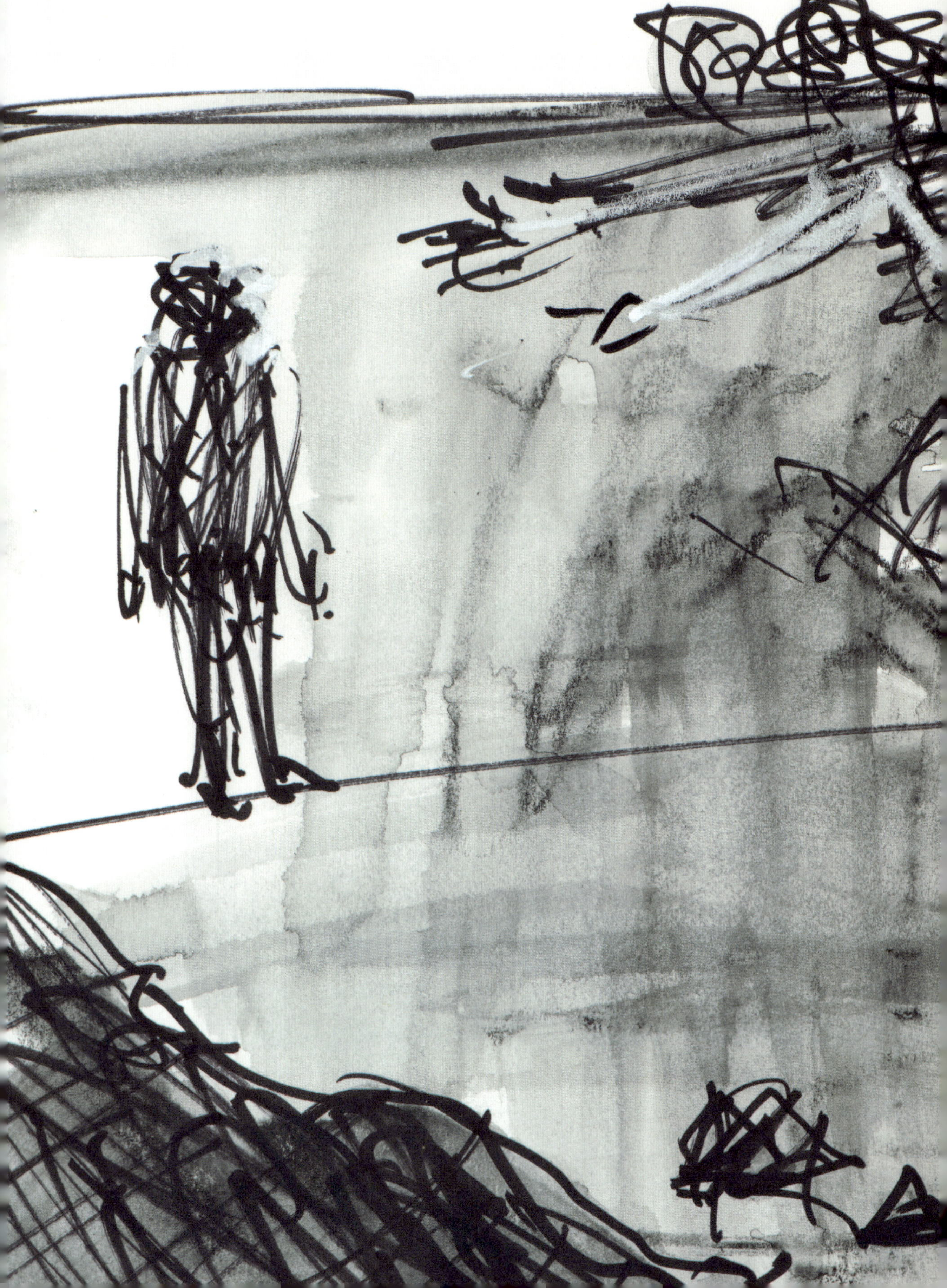

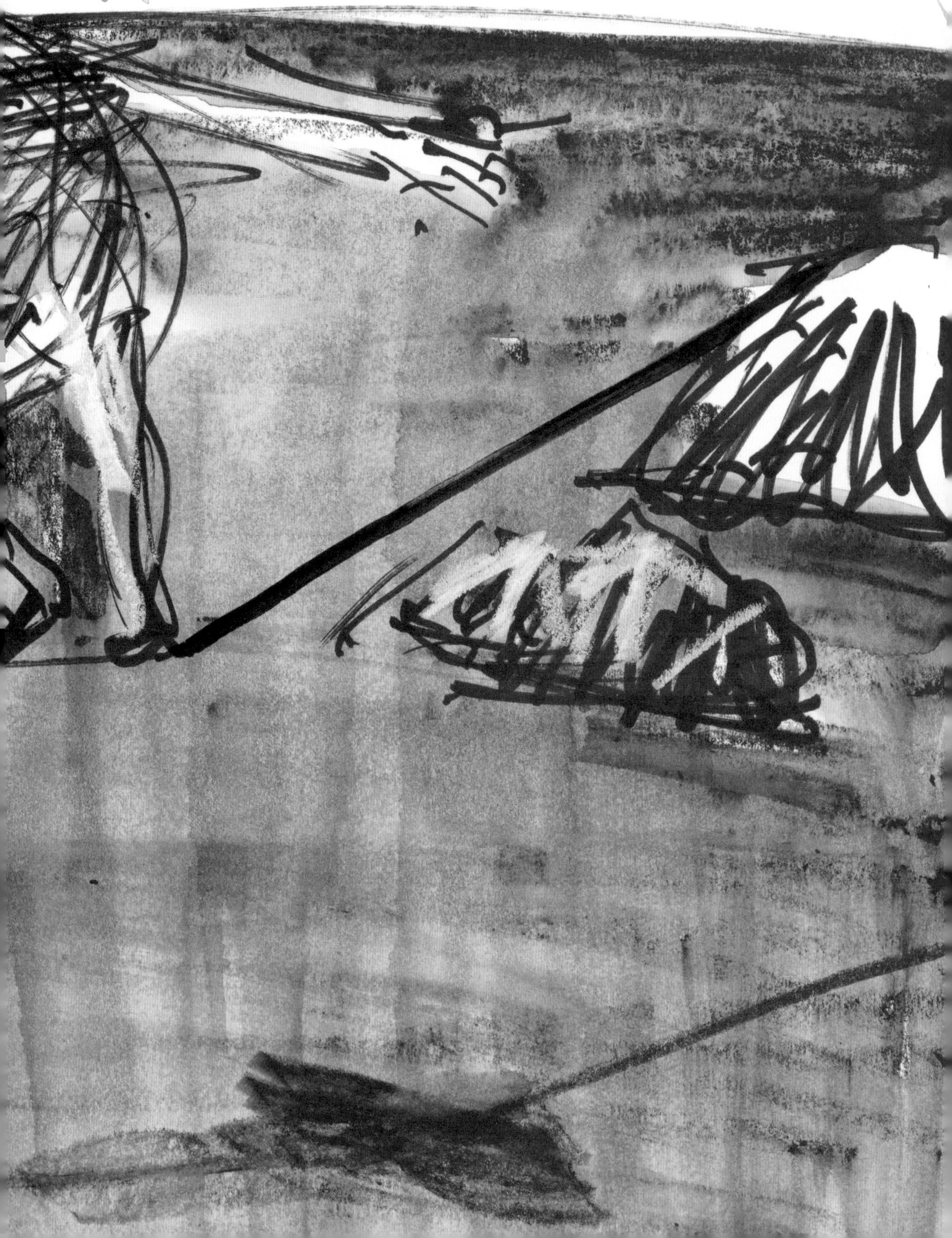

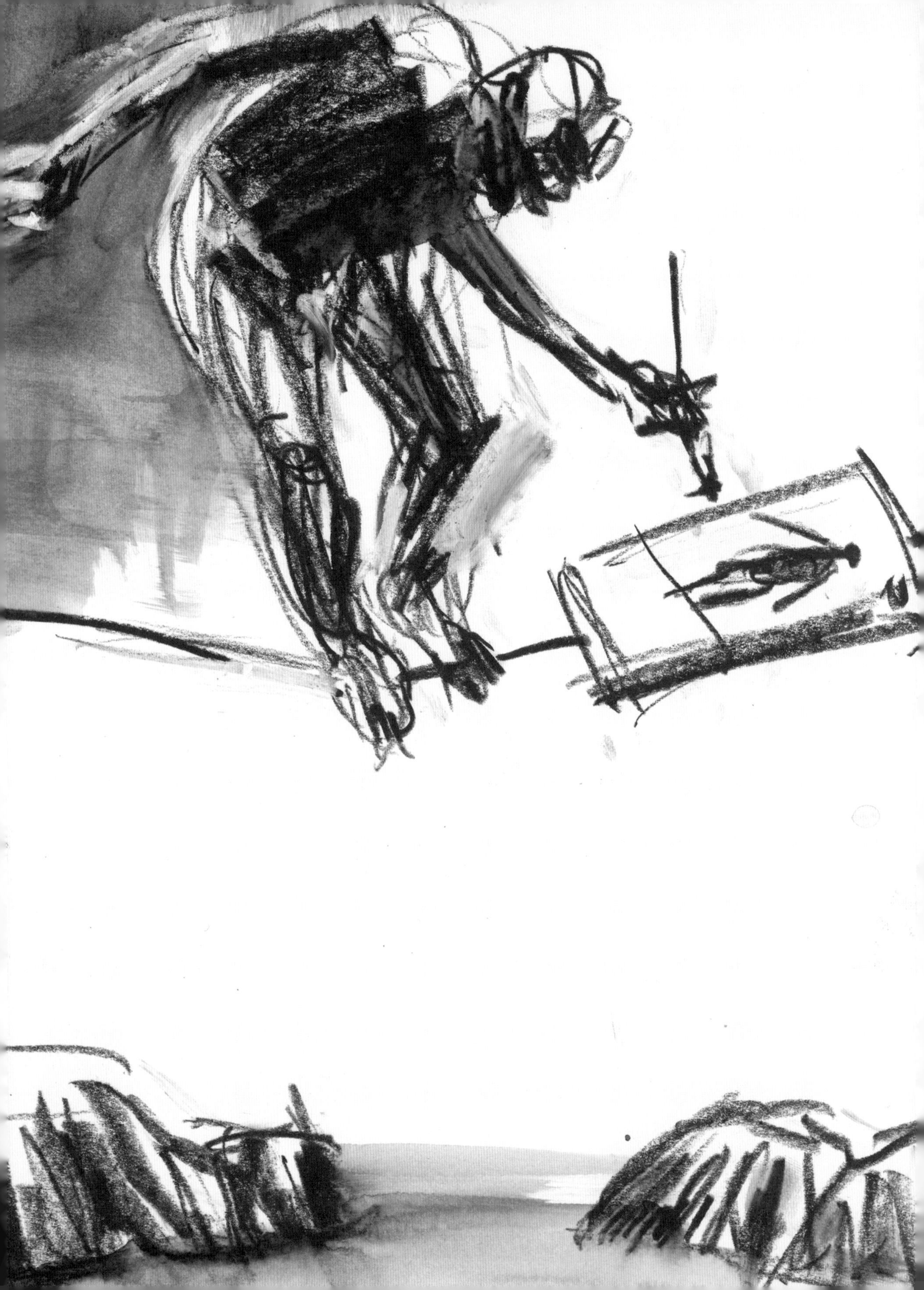

Macleod is still on a tightrope he set across years ago. He hasn't quite left. Or, to put it differently, he has still to arrive. Macleod is on a tightrope – yes, I think so. He has grown into it.

I must push on. I pack up my things, lift the pack onto my aching shoulders. Artistic dare is one thing. Belief is sustaining. If you don't, then you won't, you will fall. But at no stage did Petit wobble. He walked in the air – that's what his art demanded of him.

Words must be found. It is a new thing. And, newness springs up all around.
The journey is one of progressive naming – between here and there.

Late in the day a cloud so completely enveloped me that I experienced a kind of whiteout. I could not see. I was convinced if I stopped – that in the act of lowering my foot – I might place it down on the wrong side of the line in the sky and fall to my death.

Bridges cater to this kind of euphoria of fear: as it guarantees our passage it also creates the terror. Look at where you are – look at where you have got yourself.

Thereby transferring the blame from its engineered invitation to our own greedy natures.

For years we lived apart. Our old schedule lingered, shredded, something to grab at from time to time but not too forcefully in case it tore apart. My thoughts would shift to what she was doing at that hour — four o'clock in the afternoon, one of those empty nondescript unscheduled hours when, at last, she might be truly alone, as I and other suitors never got to see her. In another century alone with her loom or her harp or poised in deep thought over a sheet of letter-writing paper. Who might she be at that unguarded moment? We were stuck on our bank. We could not see across to her, alone at that hour.

Old *National Geographic* magazines endeavoured to colour the moment. At a time before the bridges were built, and when across the earth we lived apart, we pored over photographs we had taken of each other's strange customs.

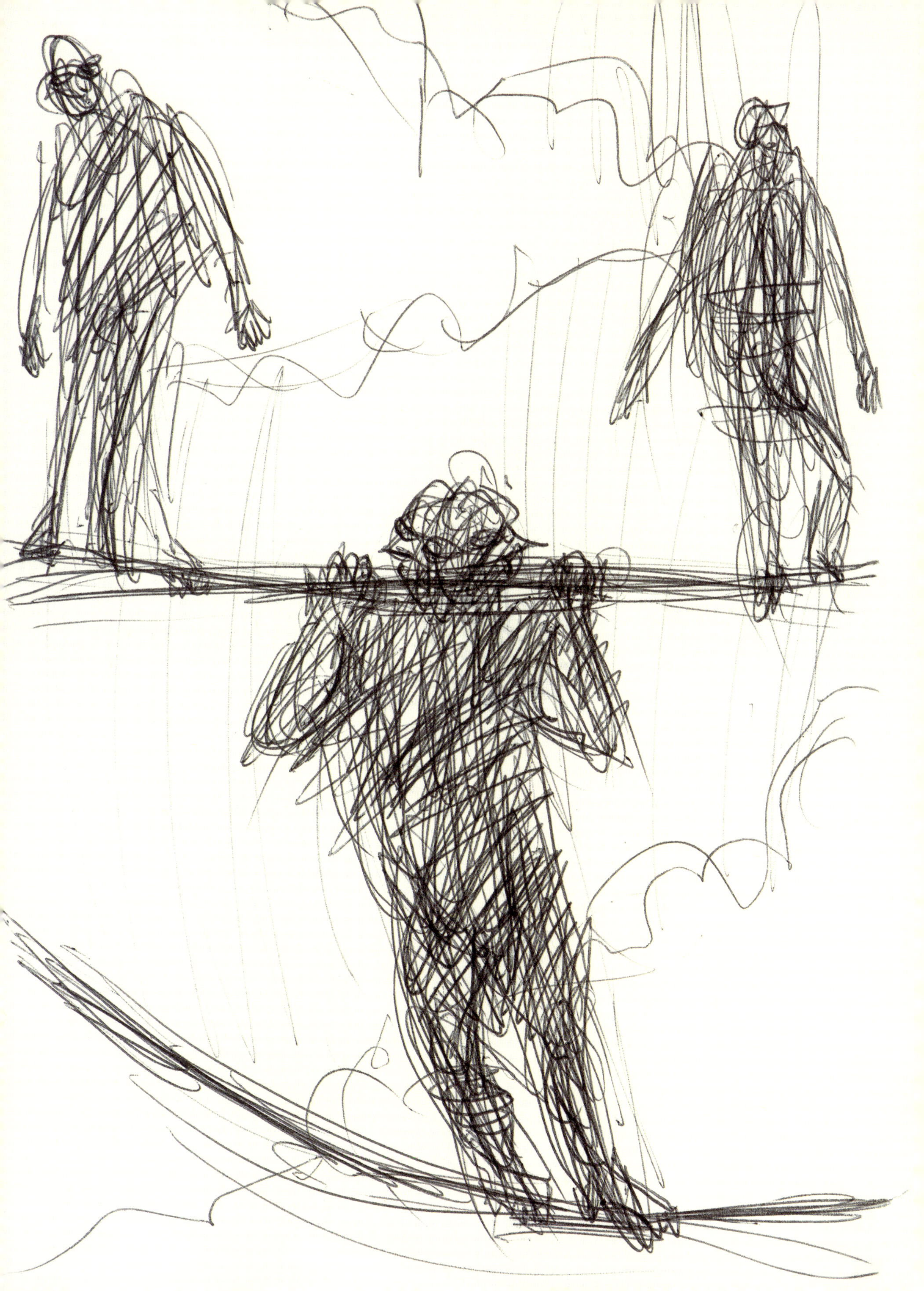

Then the bridges were built. The photographs fell into cartons. And now there is talk of detonating bridges. Sentimental talk largely by sentimentalists who recall a time when the horizon offered security. A time when they knew who they were before them over there weren't here. Local opinion is a poor match for the sophistication that built the bridges, our bare plodding feet no match for the zinc-coated beams of steel. For years we laughed at them. Mocked them, made jokes about their strange ways. Now they are our neighbours, and their sons have married our daughters. Their children won't know the time when there were bridges. They may hear about the one their family came across. But it will feel as if it belongs to a mythic time. It will feel enlarged upon, and a bit unreliable, as if the official history of the world has been placed in the hands of the regulars down at the pub.

That bridge must be kept steady and reliable, even if the place of origin will need to be re-made.

Macleod dips his brush into a familiar colour. But, familiar is now exotic. Like remembering a street filled with Humbers that is now jammed with Lime scooters and skaters in earphones. Something is wrong with the daub of paint landed on the canvas. His oval eye shifts into a line of dissatisfaction.

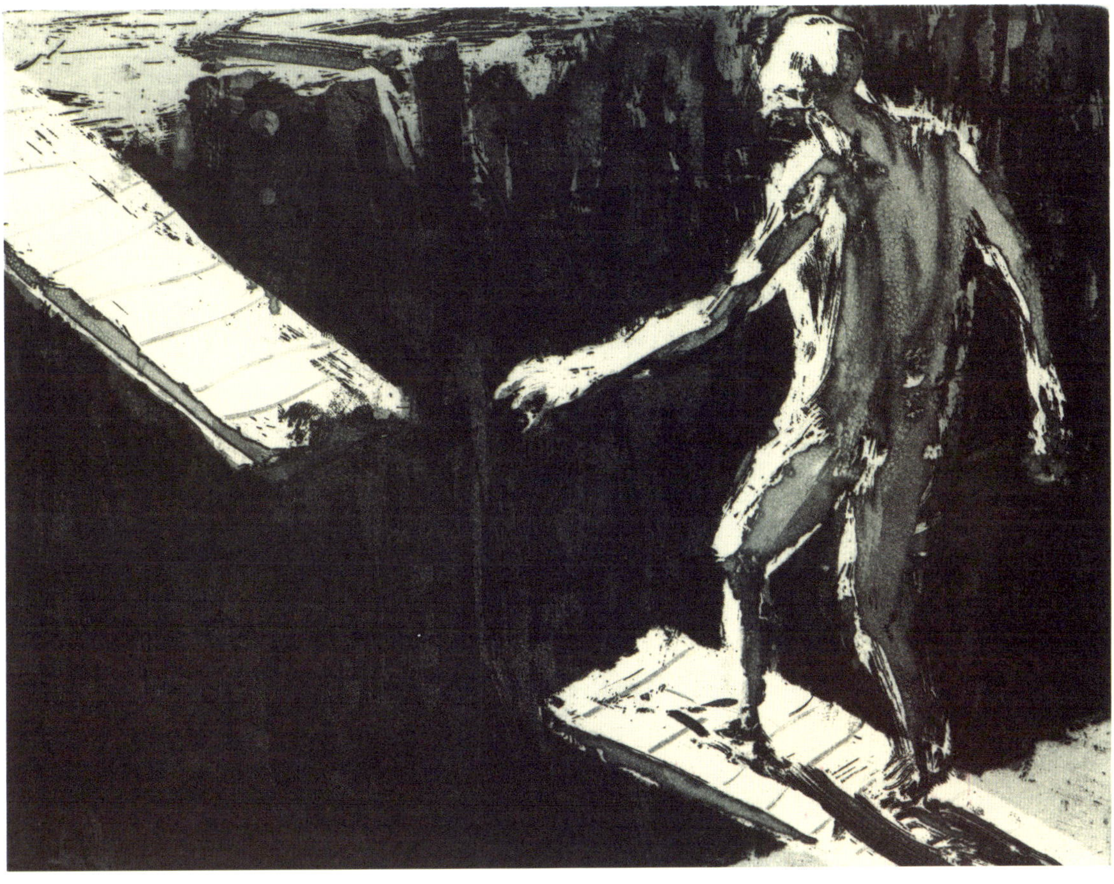

Decommissioned bridges leave a damp, sad air. The long faces of the newly divorced — flushed with hurt, eyes cast away from one another. But there was a time . . . And that sentence threads the air. The river filled with spring rain plunges on. For the river is still a thing of tumbling beauty. And if you lie down in the dry grass she may kiss you and the spans of a future will suddenly rise up before you. Here is the glorious tempting future. But, she may not. She may not kiss you, in which case the air returns to sadness and the noise is of water that is in a hurry to move on from this moment to a memory of when you leaned over the wooden balustrade — once, a long time ago — but resisted the dare of a childhood friend to jump.

In my city neighbourhood, plenty of lost souls wander the streets looking for the bridge that will get them out of here, out of Dodge, back to where they were. They don't really belong to these streets. Their bewildered eyes are proof. This morning they woke up wondering where in god's name are they? Now they are searching for that elegant rise that delivered them here. Perhaps they can travel back by the same route. Their eyes push ahead of themselves as they walk up the street. Some begin to run as the corner approaches. Then, they stop. There is no bridge. There is no bridge back to that life. Perhaps then they are in the wrong street. Perhaps the bridge is in the next street. They stagger on.

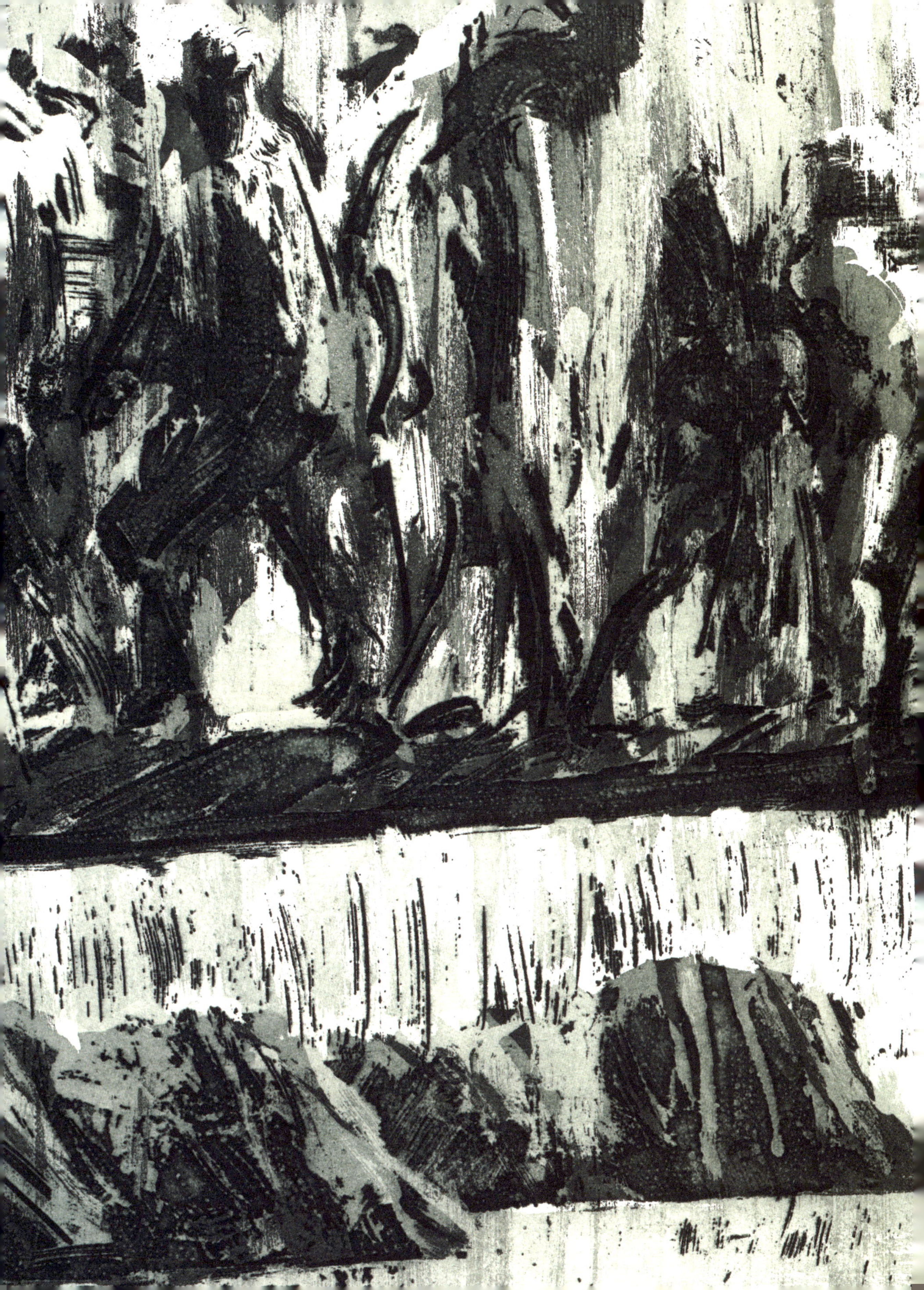

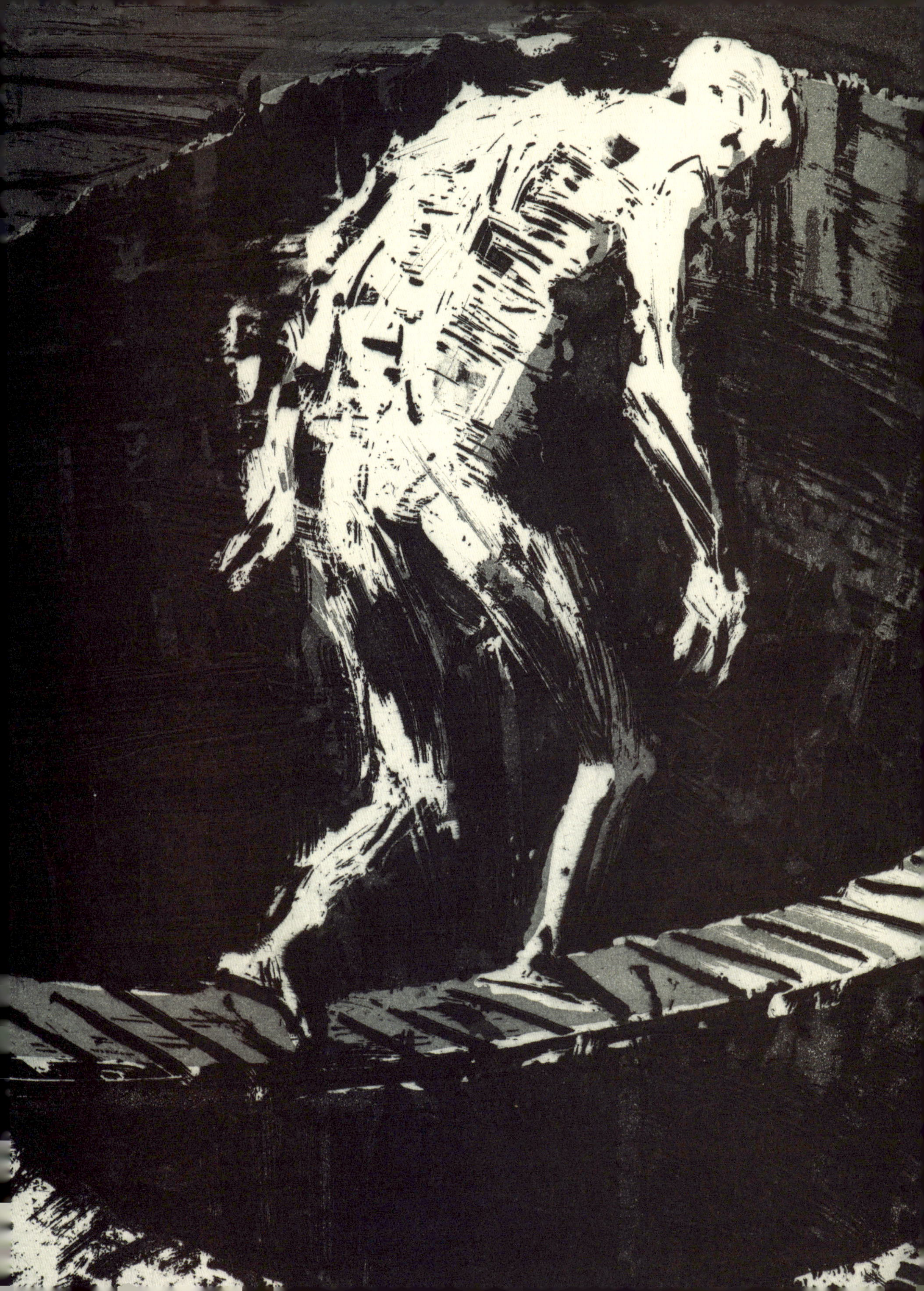

The dispiriting sound bodies make when they land on the hard road is saved for the night. This is a failing of the bridge builders. For all their engineering genius they have not been able to save us from ourselves. Our capricious souls lie outside the reach of their calculations. Rarely do we combine our certainty with a flight of madness, and one just long enough for us to imagine we are a bird, before the mistake sinks in. Our lust oozes out of us. Our tissue oozes out of us. Our residue is down to a name. Those first on the scene will look up — up into that darkness that every bridge gathers beneath it. And they make a calculation that they themselves will never act on but are helpless to prevent themselves making. Darkness and light cleave to every bridge. Except during the day when a bridge is at its most alluring and appeals to the child's rush of instant gratification.

Here, this is just for you. Rise, dear friend. Rise and follow me across to where everything will be better forever after.

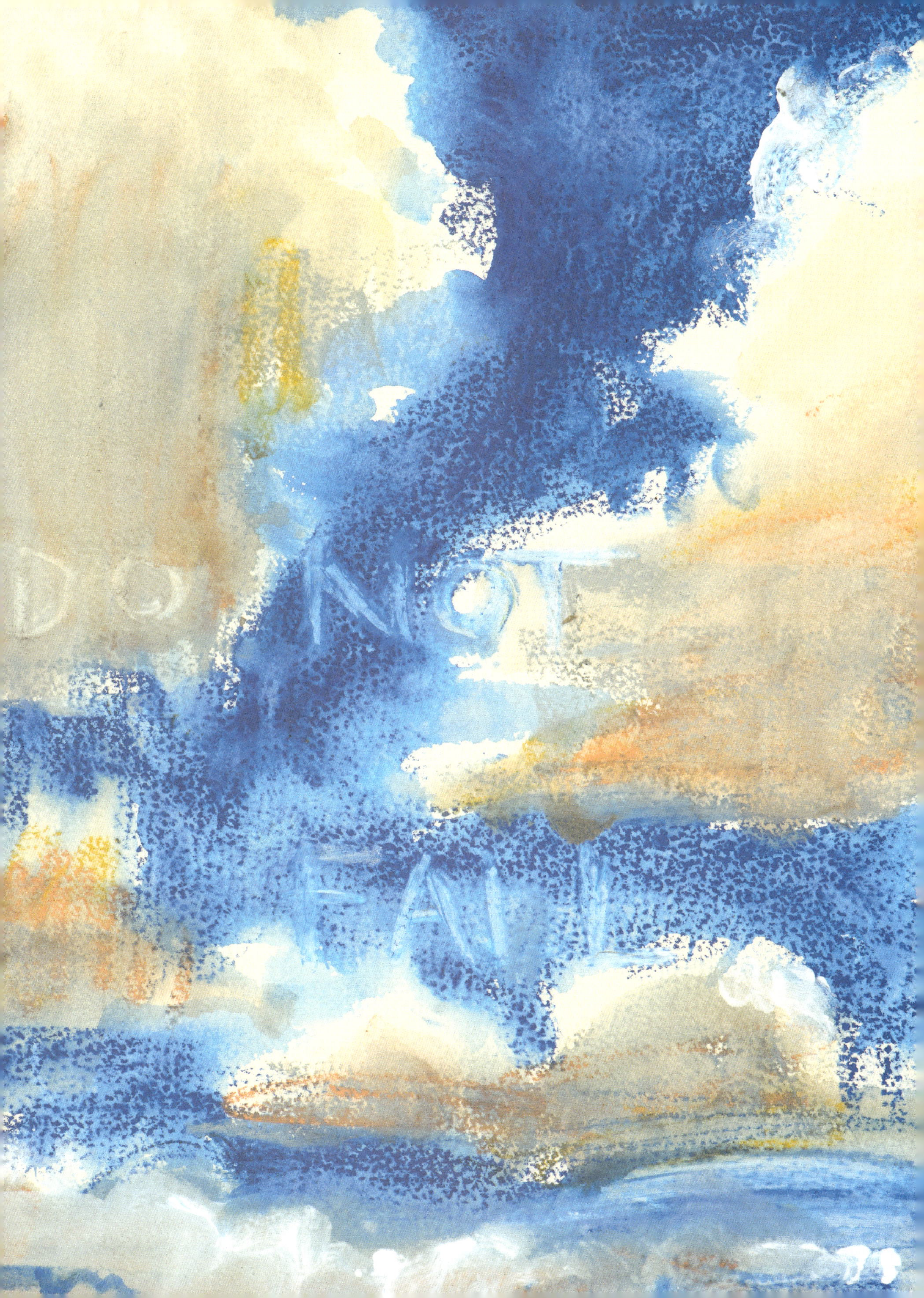
DO NOT
FAIL

Far below the blinking light of an aeroplane. The panel-beaten surface of the sea glinting and shining upwards. Far below, a fishing boat, no larger than a bath toy. But there, lining the deck, a row of upturned eyes.

It is nice to have an audience — in fact it is essential. Philippe Petit was kept aloft by our soaring hopes and fears that tore at our intestinal lining. The tightroper's composure reminded us all of who he was and who we were not. He led us into a place that we did not know existed. That is the job of any artist.

I must keep going. One foot after the other, I tell myself. Look ahead, look for what I have already seen in my mind's eye. And, surrender my flaky confidence to the single-mindedness of the bridge.

A bridge is like a forced marriage. Necessary, and evidence of a shared value system. The bridge is nothing without me. And without it I will plunge to a watery death.

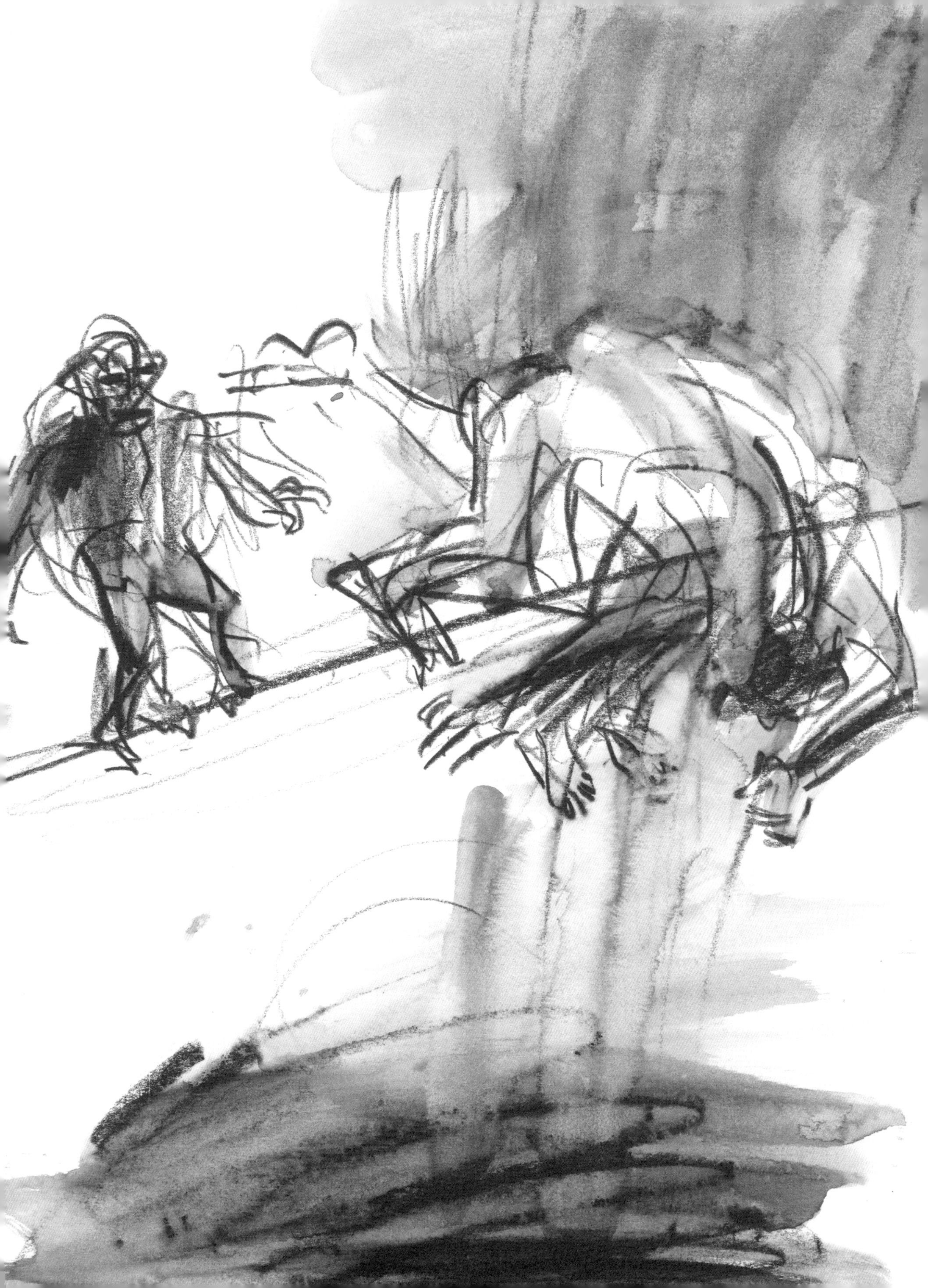

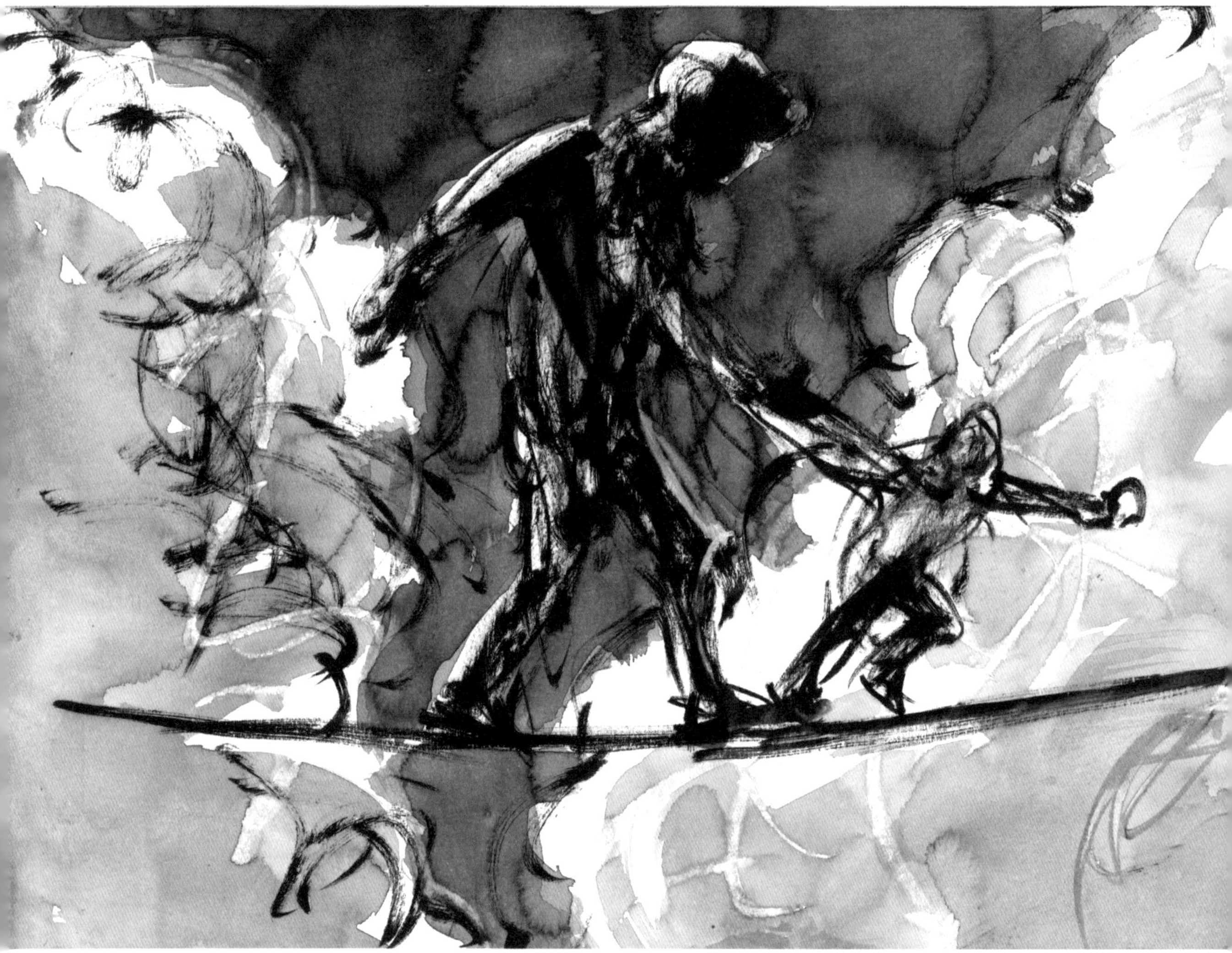

I think of the artist sketching and painting his way homeward, a lone and staggering figure hauling a bag of exotic effects after himself, presenting tall tales on his canvases – monsters under bridges, dinghies from Lyttelton Harbour hauled up on the dry sand of the Australian interior.

An island man, a singular man, washed up on a continent.

Soon I too will be straggling ashore. The end is near. I must carry on.

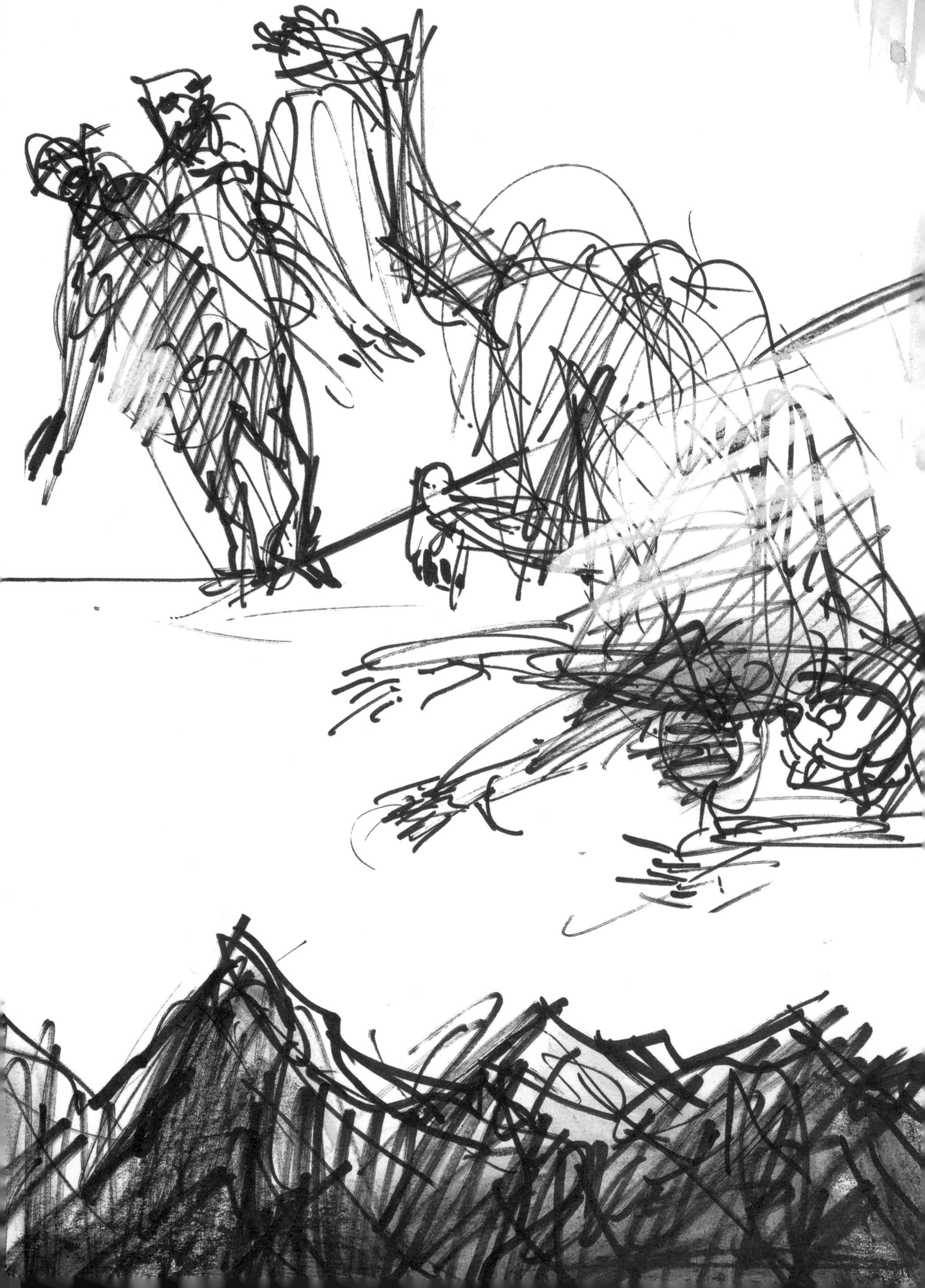

This afternoon I saw a seagull. And, towards evening, a glow as if coming from a circus tent top.

In the night I could barely sleep. The echo in the night sky was a long and low rumble.

The night fell away, and light rushed up from all directions. I got to my feet, rubbed at my eyes. There, in the distance, the red brick and the white sands of Bondi.

We may bound towards it. Or else our grip tightens on the balustrade. It has all happened too quickly. For so long out of sight — now our eyes are filled with nothing else. There it is. What we craved. Where we wished to go. Now this certainty feels like a mistake. We wonder if we were a bit rash. Still, we walk towards our bride. For that is what the future is. It is that to which we are not yet betrothed but soon will be, unless before that unifying ceremony we topple off the bridge. It happens. And I have seen it.

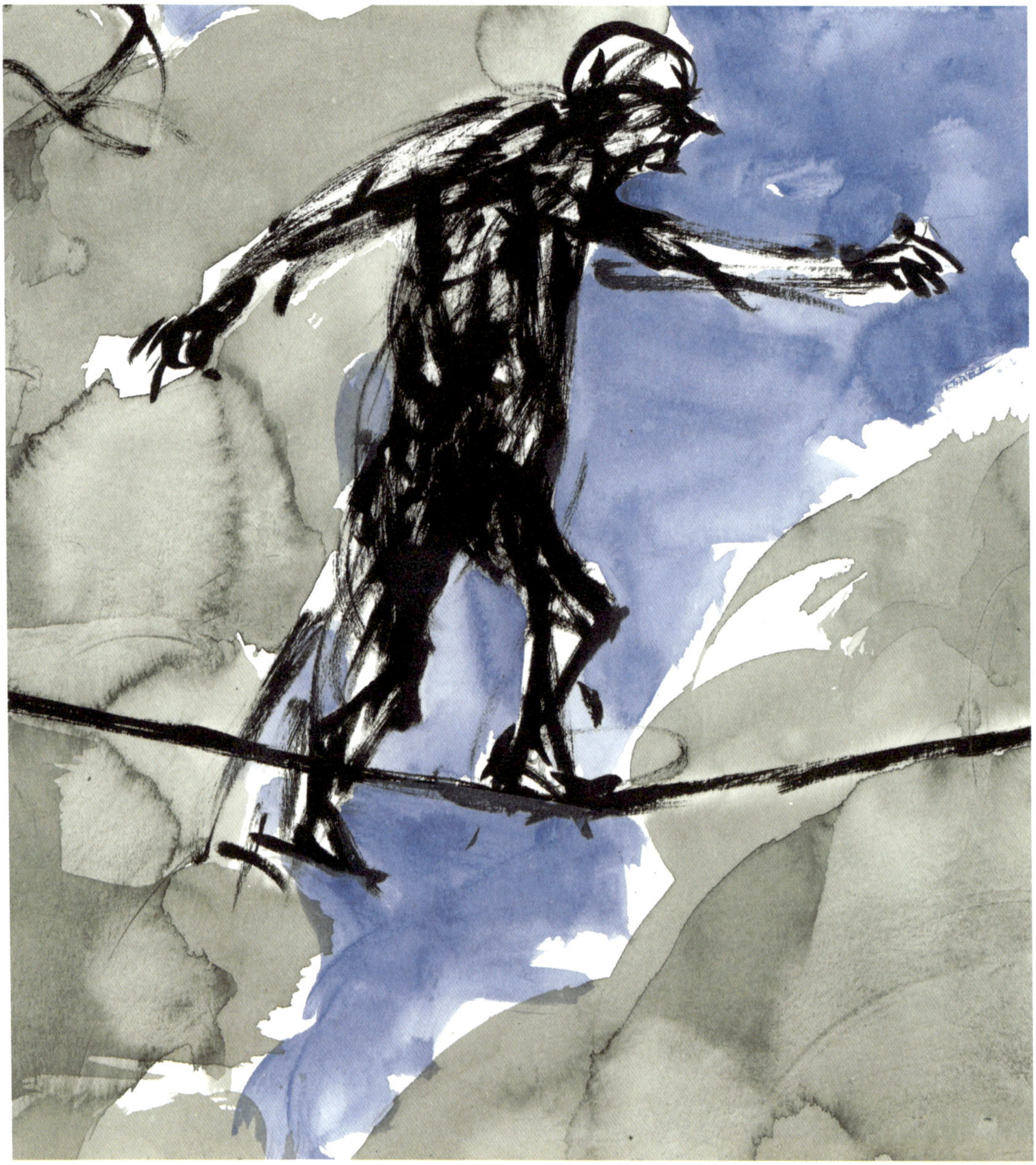

The red soil   it looks cooked
The sky is blue with a shrieking heat
I am asked to leave my woollen jersey   in the special bin
Women shelling peas a whole row of them sitting up to the bar of a pub
And I could not believe the way the younger ones lay in gutters   dresses pushed up around their heads
Like windswept flowers   the petals, I mean
The petals windswept   on race day
I'd never eaten Turkish Delight either or marzipan
Or feta, or those tiny black sheep droppings
Olives, they said
Well, I was twelve years old
I knew the sea   and the way it boomed and broke
Scattering limb

I am nearly there. It is hot, and soon I will be in the pool. There will be girls. There will be that quickening excitement in the flesh that I am still to put a name to. I may find a coin on the bottom of the pool. I did last time. The bridge is my collaborator — it too wants these things. But it wants them for me. Dear bridge.

I walked on into a gentle headwind of baked air. A tremendous rim of fire burned up into the atmosphere. I thought I'd arrived at the gates of hell. I stood and waited to be evaluated. I was surprised how compliant I seemed to be. Like Petit falling into the arms of the ridiculous New York cops after his sky walk.

As though what would happen was already known to all concerned, and all that was left to do was play our designated roles.

The line moved forward — a man took my passport, then nodded me on. Now another man intercepts me to ask if I am bringing into the country any narcotics, firearms, cash or dirt.

Temerity is not on the list.
So I am motioned to the doors marked EXIT.

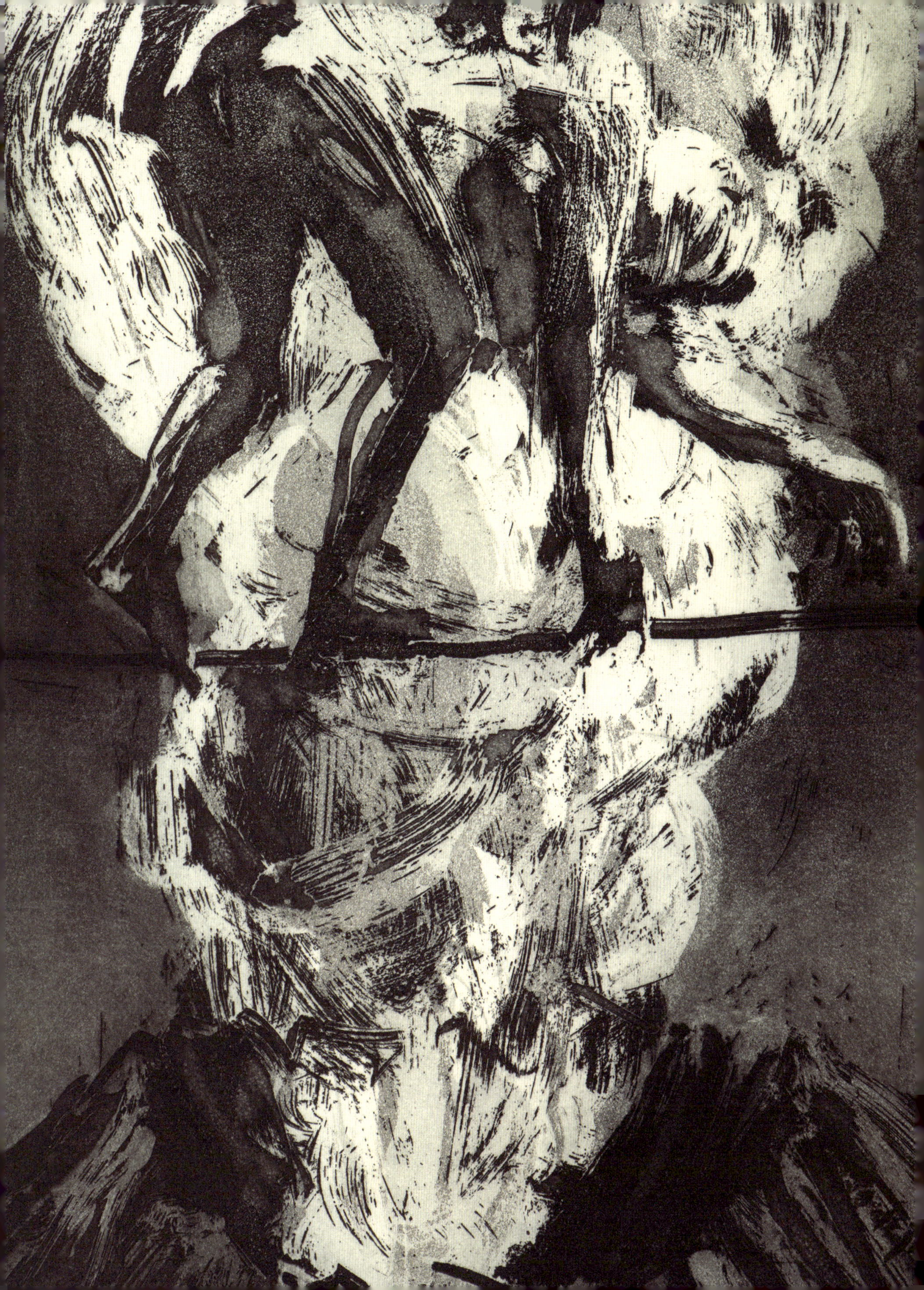

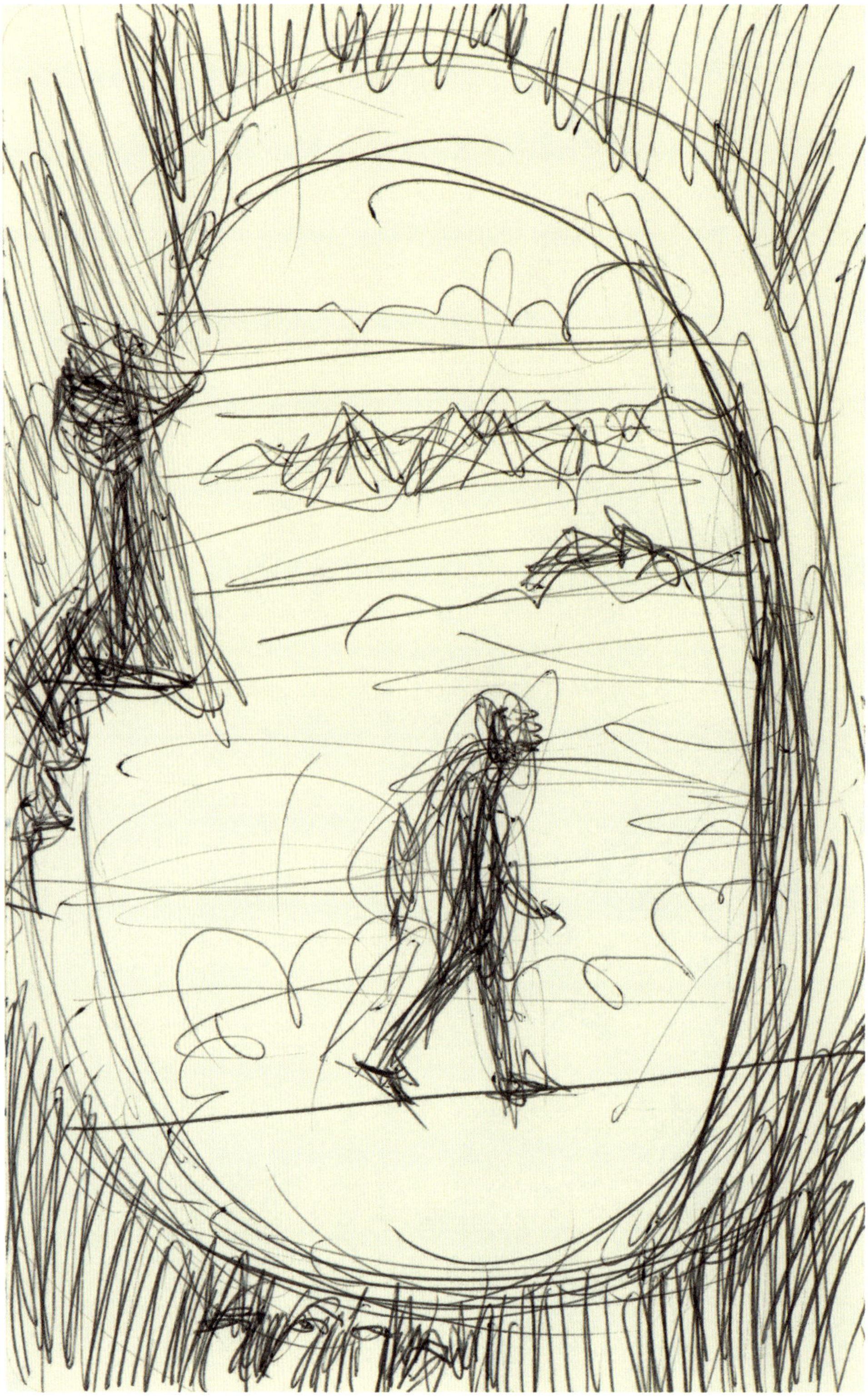

About the contributors

Lloyd Jones is a Wellington-based writer. His books include *The Book of Fame*, *Mister Pip*, *The Cage* and *A History of Silence*.

Euan Macleod was born in Christchurch and lives and works in Sydney. His work is held in many public and private collections. His awards include Australia's top prize for portraiture, the Archibald Prize.

Gary Stewart is an Otago-based designer (The Gas Project), who is well known and highly regarded for his work in book publishing.

High Wire is the first picture book in the kōrero series. The kōrero project invites new and exciting collaborations — for two different kinds of artistic intelligence to work away at a shared topic.

MASSEY UNIVERSITY PRESS

First published in 2020 by Massey University Press
Private Bag 102904, North Shore Mail Centre
Auckland 0745, New Zealand
www.masseypress.ac.nz

Design by Gary Stewart, The Gas Project
Images photographed by Michele Brouet
Cover illustration by Euan Macleod

A catalogue record for this book is available from the National Library of New Zealand

The assistance of Creative New Zealand is gratefully acknowledged by the publisher

creative nz
ARTS COUNCIL OF NEW ZEALAND TOI AOTEAROA

Printed and bound in China by Everbest Investment Ltd

ISBN: 978-0-9951230-8-3